TWISTED LOVER

Her Dangerous Obsession

Ms. Sandra Kitt—
Thank you for your
inspiration!

Len Richelle

Len Richelle

Editing & Formatting: Carla M. Dean, U Can Mark My Word
Book Cover Design: www.bookdesignstars.com
Publisher: Platinum Pen

ISBN: 978-0-9995543-0-2

PRINTED IN THE UNITED STATES OF AMERICA

Stay connected with Author Len Richelle:
authorlenrichelle.com or Facebook.com/lenrichelleauthor

To Mom:

Thank you for putting books in my hand before
I was barely able to talk. You opened an entire world to me.

Acknowledgements

To everyone in my close circle who patiently awaited the completion of this book, thank you! You heard me talk about the book, even complain about it. There were days when in frustration, I tossed it to the side and forgot about it, and thanks to you, I was reminded to keep going.

I began writing *Twisted Lover* while going through one of my darkest moments, battling breast cancer and undertaking chemotherapy. I had no plot, no goal, and no idea where the story was going, but just letting words flow to create a story was therapeutic for me—even through the toughest days of "chemo-brain" and days of hopelessness.

I'd like to give a special thanks to Stephanie Scannell-Vessella, my first beta reader and "technical" advisor. I hope my story made your train rides entertaining! Thank you, Nakesha Vines, for allowing me to share my thoughts and ideas, and helping me to piece some of the background details together. Thank you, Author Sandra Kitt, one of my most inspiring writers, for the creative writing workshop. Someday, I'll travel to St. John for new creative inspo! Thank you, Author Christine Meade, for your fiction workshops and teaching me how to exercise the power of writing! Most of all, I thank God for giving me life and allowing me to find my passion in the world of writing.

Peace and Love to all of you!

Len Richelle

TWISTED LOVER

Her Dangerous Obsession

Chapter One
The Interview

Adrienne worried she wouldn't make it on time. Sitting on the cramped city bus, she stared out the window to distract herself from the intense anxiety that crept upon her. She wished the bus would move faster through the busy New Rochelle neighborhoods. Her interview was 9:00 A.M., and she would still have to walk three blocks from the bus stop. The customer service position she applied for was not her first choice; she had no interest in the insurance business, and most of all, she dreaded the thought of having to take a bus to work every day. However, it was only one of two interviews she was called for, and she desperately needed the summer job to buy new clothes before returning to college.

By the time she reached her stop, she had ten minutes to get to the office. Her three-inch Michael Kors heels were not meant for fast walking on the hard pavement, and with the early morning heatwave, she could feel the sweat rolling down the middle of her back underneath her navy-blue Calvin Klein suit. Adrienne always had a taste for designer fashion, and she would use her summer-job money for just that. Each year, when she came home from college, she worked long hours, only to spend her checks on designer labels. "You should be saving your money for school," her mother often said. Adrienne paid no attention to her mom's advice. Her goal was to show up on campus dressed in the latest fashion. To her, designer clothes were everything.

I hope my curls didn't flop. Adrienne brushed the front tresses of hair away from her eyes as she hurried up the front steps of the building. Before entering the double glass doors, she took a quick look at her reflection. *Curls still in place. I'm good.*

A receptionist behind the front desk greeted her.

"Good morning. May I help you?" asked the woman.

The young lady was not much older than Adrienne. She wore a naturally curly hairstyle and large, colorful dangling earrings. She peered through a pair of oversized, black-rimmed glasses that almost covered half of her face.

"Yes, I…umm…have an interview. I'm Adrienne Madison."

Adrienne clung tightly to the strap of her purse with one hand while the sweaty palm of her other hand gripped the folder holding her résumé.

"Sure. Have a seat over there, and I'll let someone know you're here."

Adrienne took a seat in the small waiting area to the left of the receptionist's desk. Glancing around, she noticed the rich décor, which indicated a thriving business. A wall fountain directly behind the receptionist's desk gave the waiting area a relaxing and tranquil feel, and mahogany walls matched the wood on the elegantly-styled furniture. *Hmm, I could enjoy this all day.* Soft jazz played through the overhead speakers, and a refreshing, aromatherapy scent permeated the air. Even the receptionist's workstation looked like a presidential suite with its high-back leather swivel chair and glass shelving that displayed ceramic vases filled with beautiful green plants. So far, Adrienne was impressed.

"Adrienne?" the middle-aged woman called to her, coming to greet her.

"Hi, nice to meet you." Adrienne quickly stood up to shake the hand of the tall, thin woman, who gave a half-smile and inclined her head.

Her name was Paula, and she was the office manager who would also be Adrienne's direct supervisor. While following Paula through the corridor leading to her office, Adrienne noticed her rigid demeanor as she interacted with other staff members passing by. Paula wore a red blazer with big gold buttons, a colorful maxi skirt, and flat black shoes. Her hair was pulled back into a tight bun, and she wore a set of red-framed glasses on top of her head. Her less-than-cordial personality gave Adrienne the impression that Paula was formal and all about business.

"So, how are you enjoying your summer so far?" asked Paula.

She barely cracked a smile, and Adrienne got the impression the small talk was just a formality.

"It's fine. I've only been home a few days from school, but I'm enjoying the time off."

"And how long before you return to college?"

"Not until the middle of August," said Adrienne. "I hope that won't be a problem."

"No, not at all. After all, this is a summer job. It's usually available for an intern interested in working in the insurance business, but we needed a little extra help this year with having a couple of our staff out for various reasons." Paula sighed and waved her hand as if the hiring process was a hopeless case. "Any help will do."

Her bland expression didn't change as she let out a deep sigh. Adrienne wondered if it was because she was tired of interviewing so many applicants or if this was her personality all the time. She was already nervous about the interview, and

Paula's cold attitude wasn't helping. The fact that Adrienne had no interest in the insurance business didn't boost her motivation to try as hard as she could during the interview. At that moment, Adrienne just wanted to get the whole thing over with.

After small talk, Paula began by asking Adrienne more relevant questions pertaining to her work skills. Adrienne responded nervously and often stuttered with each response. She couldn't remember even the most basic answers about herself and her past customer service experience.

Damn, I'm screwing up. She had a feeling she made a terrible impression with Paula and expected to be dismissed immediately after the interview. However, Paula surprised her with an offer to continue the process.

"I would like you to meet our CEO, Mr. Weathers. He'll give you a brief interview. Do you have time to stay?"

Adrienne reluctantly followed Paula further down the hall. *What could I possibly say to the company's CEO that would impress him? Besides, I'm hungry.*

They passed a station of cubicles where several staff members wearing earpieces talked to clients on the other end of the line.

"This is our customer service department," Paula said as she pointed toward the group of employees.

Everyone was so focused on their calls that none of them bothered looking up to acknowledge the ladies as they passed by. Adrienne followed Paula as she turned down another hall to a quieter area. The hallway led to a large office with glass double doors. Inside was a man sitting behind a large mahogany wood desk staring at the computer in front of him. Paula tapped lightly on the door, then walked in with Adrienne timidly following behind.

"Mr. Weathers, I'd like you to meet one of our applicants, Ms. Adrienne Madison."

When Mr. Weathers stood up, Adrienne nearly lost her

breath. She was instantly attracted to the 6'2" man in his late thirties with smooth, caramel-colored skin. His freshly cut hair showed off his natural waves, and his neatly trimmed goatee complemented his squared jawbone. He reminded Adrienne of one of the sexy models in magazines showing off their chiseled bodies, except the man standing in front of her was fully dressed. Her eyes quickly moved from head to toe, and although she didn't know much about menswear, she could tell he was wearing an expensive, custom-fitted suit. *Business must be doing very well.*

Mr. Weathers held out his hand, and Adrienne placed her hand gently in his. The strong yet soft feel of his grip gave her a slightly tingling feeling inside. She didn't notice that Paula had stepped out of the office. She was too enamored with the handsome man in front of her.

"You can call me Daron. Please, have a seat." He motioned for her to sit in a burgundy cushioned chair, never taking his eyes off her.

While he scanned her résumé, Adrienne glanced around the room. There were framed certificates, awards, and several pictures of him and other men in suits who looked very important. She perked up and watched him as he sat across the desk, nodding his head in approval. Daron then began his interview.

He was very inquisitive about her work and college experience, and unlike Paula's interview, Mr. Weathers made Adrienne feel comfortable enough to talk about herself. She liked that he asked her questions about hobbies, likes, and dislikes. When she discovered they shared some of the same interests, the conversation got even better.

"Oh, so you were a Jeter fan, huh? I don't know too many women who weren't." Mr. Weathers chuckled as Adrienne defended her favorite Yankee player.

She looked in Mr. Weathers' dreamy eyes as he ran off stats and compared a few other former players he thought were more impressive. The conversation turned from business to fun as the two shared their interests and backgrounds.

Adrienne was comfortable talking to Daron almost immediately, sharing things about her life most people she just met wouldn't know for a long time.

"I live with my mother and younger sister, Kara," she said casually. "Kara will be going to the eleventh grade next year, while I'll be entering my senior year of college." She glimpsed around the office and admired the details of the fancy décor before adding, "After that, I'll probably go for my master's and maybe work in…insurance."

Adrienne coyly looked up at Daron to see if her sudden enthusiasm about the insurance business impressed him.

Daron chuckled. "I can appreciate that, Ms. Madison."

"Oh, please call me Adrienne."

"All right, Adrienne. That's a deal. As long as you call me Daron."

The two of them maintained eye contact for a moment, staring at each other in silence. Then Daron cleared his throat and continued with the interview. He shifted to a more serious demeanor as he discussed the duties of the position in more detail. Adrienne listened as she watched each word flow from Daron's soft, moist lips. The alluring tone of his sensual voice gently sang into her ears. As he spoke, Adrienne fantasized about their future lives together.

We own the insurance company together, and as his wife and partner, I become the new office manager because Paula is fired. I will manage the office's day-to-day operations as he rakes in profits from million-dollar accounts. At the end of every workday, we ride home together in one of our many luxury cars to our beautiful mansion, where dinner will be served to us by a personal chef.

It was an enjoyable twenty-five-minute interview, and Adrienne nodded attentively as Daron proudly boasted about the highlights of his company. He built it from the ground up,

14

he said. He worked for an insurance agency after graduating from a university in Connecticut. *Oh, my school is in Connecticut, too.* He owed his success to his former boss, his mentor who taught him everything. Adrienne was mesmerized by this handsome, intelligent, and highly successful man sitting in front of her, and in her head, she prayed he would hire her on the spot. *I will be his best employee. He'll fall in love with me. I can be Mrs. Weathers.*

Adrienne laughed at herself—planning, plotting, and scheming when she hadn't yet been offered the job. As the interview came to an end, she couldn't wait to go home to continue daydreaming about her new crush. That is until he clasped his hands together and placed them on top of the desk. The sparkle of the diamonds in his white gold wedding band reflected brightly into her eyes. Her heart sank.

*****

Adrienne arrived home later that morning with hopeful thoughts that she would get the job. If she had only interviewed with Paula, she knew her chances of getting the position were slim. After all, she stuttered when providing answers and couldn't elaborate on half the skills listed on her résumé. Now all she could do was hope the instant connection she had with Daron would be her saving chance.

That evening, she had dinner with her mother and younger sister, Kara. Adrienne was more than excited to talk about the job interview when her mother asked about it.

"Slow down, Ade. You're talking so fast. It sounds like it's something you really want to do. I thought that job was the last one on your list."

"Yes, but now that I got to know a little more about it, I think I could be interested in the insurance business."

Adrienne wouldn't dare tell her mother the real reason was because of her potential boss. If she had, her mom would have probably discouraged her from taking the job if it was offered. For now, Adrienne would keep her reasons for her sudden interest in the insurance business to herself. Daron would be her little secret.

*****

6:32 P.M.

"It's been a long day, Paula," said Daron.

He stretched his arms up and clasped his hands behind his head. Paula, his office manager, sat directly in front of him, pen and pad in hand, taking notes.

"Yes, it has been," Paula replied while trying to hold in a yawn as she continued scribbling notes on the pad.

The two of them had been staying late the last few days while trying to make decisions on hiring new applicants.

"So, who do you think are our top three candidates? I think that gentleman, George, is excellent for the position," said Paula.

She peered over her red-framed glasses and waited for Daron's approval. He appeared to be in deep thought as he stared into mid-air.

"Mr. Weathers? Daron? Hello?" said Paula in a loud tone, then looked at her watch. *Why doesn't this man ever want to go home?*

"Huh? Oh, he's good, but he's looking for something permanent. This is only a summer position. We hire him, and he'll have to look for something else in a couple of months."

Only two other applicants were worth considering. Paula cringed at the idea of hiring either one. The first had some experience, but, Paula didn't think she would fit in personality-wise. The second one was a college student with no experience in the insurance business. She seemed pretty bright, but Paula didn't find her assertive enough for the position. Besides, there

16

was something else about her that raised a red flag. The applicant reminded her of a woman who may stir something in Daron. Paula couldn't put her finger on it, but she knew Adrienne Madison was trouble from the word go. Paula would discourage Daron's desire to hire her. There was just too much temptation there.

"I think I'd like to hire Adrienne Madison," said Daron.

He sat up in his chair and slapped his palm on his desk as if to confirm his decision. Paula looked at him in dismay. She knew it wasn't a good idea. Adrienne was probably a very smart girl, but the more she thought about it, the more she saw an oddly striking resemblance of Daron's wife, Linda. A younger version, but still very close.

Doesn't he see that? Oh, maybe he does.

"I don't think I agree, Daron. I just don't think… I don't think she has the experience we're looking for," Paula said, choosing her words carefully.

Daron leaned over in his chair to get a closer look at her face, and in a stern voice, he interrupted her.

"Paula, remember, *I* make the final decisions here."

It wasn't the first time he had snapped at her. Something had been irritating him for a while now. Paula dropped her head to a spot on the floor; she felt embarrassed and angry. Having worked for Daron since he first started the company, she knew his wife and respected the couple very much. Paula had seen a lot of things going on within the company and always knew when Daron was making the wrong decision. This time was one of them.

"Yes, sir, of course," Paula said.

She continued to scribble on her pad as Daron gave her further instructions—check references, call Adrienne, ask her to start on Monday. Paula finished taking notes and then left, walking down the empty hallway. *Well, we'll see if he knows what he's doing,* she thought to herself. She headed to her office, gathered her belongings, and headed out the door, leaving Daron swiveling in his chair.

About half an hour later, Daron grabbed his briefcase and headed out, as well. On the drive home, he thought about the new employee he had just hired and smiled. Adrienne reminded him of a younger version of Linda. There was so much resemblance that Daron even questioned himself about the real reason he hired her. The thought of hiring her made him feel slightly guilty. He thought about George, the more qualified applicant. *The brother does need a job.* But Daron quickly shook off his guilty feelings and continued home.

Twenty minutes later, Daron pulled into his home garage and walked inside. The scent of Linda's perfume was in the air. He stopped in the kitchen to find it as clean as that morning before he left for work. *She must have just gotten home. Looks like we'll be ordering take-out.* He walked up the stairs to the bedroom to find Linda frantically pulling clothes out from her closet.

"What's going on, babe?" asked Daron.

"They've asked me to speak at a luncheon in Ohio tomorrow. It's a last-minute thing, but I said yes. I'm taking an early flight, and I've got to finish working on my speech tonight."

Linda didn't bother looking up as she continued pulling her clothes from the rack. Daron sat on the bed next to the half-full suitcase and watched Linda toss her belongings inside.

"So, you're just going to leave? Just like that?" asked Daron.

Feeling the heat rise on the back of his neck, he loosened his collar. It wasn't the first time Linda pulled a last-minute trip like this. He looked forward to having a nice dinner with his wife tonight, followed by a hot shower and hopefully sex. *Yeah, it's been a while since that happened.* So far, the chances of both ideas seemed slim to none.

"Well, I'll have dinner delivered. What would you like?" he said.

"You can get what you want. I already ate before I came home. Thanks, babe."

Daron sat quietly as Linda continued packing without ever making eye contact with him. Realizing he was fighting a losing battle, he walked into his closet and took off his suit. Wearing only his t-shirt and boxers, he went back downstairs to find something to eat. It looked like it was going to be another lonely night. Whenever Linda prepared for one of her many trips, it was all about her.

After eating leftovers, Daron jumped in the shower and then got in the bed. By now, Linda had finished packing and was downstairs in her office working on her speech for the next day.

"I'll wait up for you," Daron said, "but don't take too long. Okay, babe?"

He wanted to spend time with her before her trip and tried hard to stay awake until she finished working on her speech. However, when he woke up the next morning, he found the other side of the bed empty.

She did it again.

Daron jerked back the covers to get out of bed and dressed for work. He was furious that Linda left without saying goodbye.

She didn't even wake me to make love last night.

Linda had been so busy with her book promotions, traveling all over the country, and spending so much time in her office writing new books that she spent very little time with Daron. Her bestsellers brought her into the limelight, and Daron felt neglected.

"Babe, we're making good money now. Why don't you slow down a little with your book tours?" he once asked Linda. It was another night of packing before one of her book tours.

"Oh, Daron, can we please discuss this when I'm not so stressed out? You know how I am when I'm getting ready for these events!" Linda continued packing her suitcase while

Len Richelle

Daron quietly sat on the bed watching. His glimpse of hope of a happier marriage was slowly dwindling.

Chapter Two
The New Girl

As soon as Adrienne received the call from Paula offering her the job, she went straight to the mall to shop for work clothes. Adrienne didn't know if she was more excited about getting the job or having a chance to see Daron again. However, as she picked out each suit and coordinating blouse from the racks, she carefully selected them with Daron in mind.

He'll love me in this, she thought, admiring herself in the royal-blue pencil skirt and low-cut powder blue silk blouse.

She smiled in the mirror and leaned over just enough to allow her gold heart pendant to dangle from her cleavage. She licked her lips seductively while imagining herself reviewing files with Daron in a dimly lit office. There were so many tricks she had up her sleeve to get Daron's attention that she couldn't wait to start working at the office. Adrienne tried on each outfit as she role-played each scenario in her head. She carefully selected colors and shades that complemented her skin tone and chose the styles that only showed off her curves. She knew the outfits would meet Daron's approval and couldn't wait to model each of them around him. Then suddenly, her fantasy came to an abrupt halt when she remembered the shiny wedding band that adorned his finger. *He's still cute, though.*

By Monday morning, Adrienne was a nervous wreck. It was difficult starting a new job, especially when it came to meeting new people. Being an introvert, Adrienne didn't typically make friends right away, and at this new job, it somehow seemed to be harder than usual. Most of the staff were women, and Adrienne appeared to be the youngest. Right away, Paula gave her a tour of the office while introducing her to everyone, then sat her down next to Phyllis, the one who would be training her in customer service.

Phyllis was in her mid-fifties and had been with the company for about five years. Her overly dyed hair showed various shades of blond and was tightly pinned in an updo style. She reeked of an old perfume that reminded Adrienne of one of her elderly high school teachers. It was apparent Phyllis was happy to have someone share the workload. As soon as Adrienne sat down, she began quoting a list of instructions. While she spoke, she reached over to a shelf behind her and pulled out a pile of folders that she handed to Adrienne.

"These are your accounts. Just do everything I just explained."

Although Adrienne was usually a quick learner, she had been a little distracted during Phyllis' instructions. She looked forward to seeing Daron again and kept looking up every time she heard someone coming down the hall. She couldn't wait to get a glimpse of him that morning.

"Did you get that?" Phyllis asked, seeing that Adrienne seemed to be distracted.

"Huh? Oh, yes, I got it," Adrienne said. She sat back in her chair and felt her face turn red. *Focus, Adrienne.*

"All right, girl. Don't let me waste my time here," Phyllis mumbled.

Adrienne watched as Phyllis arranged a batch of paperwork. She suddenly stopped and gave Adrienne another look, then waved at her to go work on the files at her own desk.

"Well, go on," she said.

"Okay," Adrienne replied. "Uh, thank you, Phyllis."

Adrienne could tell Phyllis was frustrated with her. She couldn't blame her. She just spent the last hour explaining the basics of her job, and Adrienne didn't hear a word.

*****

It wasn't long after Adrienne began her assignment that she heard his voice. Her heart raced as the sound of his smooth, sensual tone rang through the halls until it reached her department.

"Good morning, everyone. How's it going?" Daron bellowed as he continued down the aisle.

He moved his head side-to-side, making sure to greet as many employees as possible. Adrienne quickly patted her hair and used her cellphone camera to check her lipstick. There he was. Tall, handsome, and beaming with all his sexiness.

"Good morning, Phyllis. Heyyy, Adrienne. Good to see you."

His smile was enough to make Adrienne melt, and she grinned from ear to ear as he disappeared down the hall.

At lunchtime, Phyllis took Adrienne out to the courtyard, where they joined some of the other employees to eat. It was a beautiful seating area with flowerbeds and a streaming fountain. Adrienne was impressed. Her new boss really knew how to treat his staff.

She followed Phyllis to one of the picnic tables, where a few ladies were already eating. After introducing themselves, Adrienne joined them with her lunch. A couple of the ladies asked her a few questions—where she attended school, what was her major, where was she from, etc. Adrienne proudly responded, hoping to impress them with the good school she attended and her aspirations of obtaining her MBA. Adrienne was intelligent, and people were often impressed with her achievements. She hoped to talk a little more about herself; however, after only a few questions, the women turned their interest back to their group conversation, leaving Adrienne out of the loop and feeling awkward. She listened attentively and wanted to join in the discussion but had no idea who Adele was from Accounting and missed Javier's retirement party to agree on how delicious the pasta was or how great Miranda looked since recovering from her surgery. Feeling out of place, she drifted from the conversations and kept an eye on the courtyard entrance, hoping to get another glimpse of Daron.

*****

The following day, Daron walked through the area about the same time, speaking to and smiling at the employees. Adrienne looked up to see him wearing a dark navy-blue suit, a silver tie, and an expensive pair of black Gucci loafers.

"Hey Adrienne, I hope everything is going well," Daron addressed her.

He had left her with her mouth open and caught off guard.

"Yes…everything…is fine," she stammered.

"You let me know if you need anything," Daron tossed over his shoulder as he left the area.

The other women were watching Adrienne and her reaction to Daron.

"Here's another one that's been mesmerized by bossman," Rhonda mumbled but loud enough for Adrienne to hear.

She chuckled and pointed at Adrienne while the other women began to laugh, too. Embarrassed, Adrienne dropped her head.

"Girl, you don't have to be embarrassed. There's not a woman here who didn't do the same thing when they first got hired. It'll pass. He's in love with his wife and is not interested in any other woman," Monique told her.

Adrienne didn't respond. She just wanted the ground to open up and swallow her whole. What Adrienne didn't say and would keep to herself was that Daron may not have had an interest in any of them, but he would definitely have an interest in her. She would see to that.

Chapter Three

Gone Are the Days

Daron watched as she smoothed out her dress and turned around several times while looking in the full-length mirror. The burgundy dress was one of his favorites––low-cut in the front, tight-fitting, and showing off the curves he couldn't wait to get his hands on. He walked up from behind and pressed up against her. His arms wrapped low around her waist. He knew she felt his hardness damn near pushing through the back of her dress. She closed her eyes and tilted her head while he glided his tongue softly down her neck.

"Mmm," Linda moaned. "You're going to make us late."

It was another night out with David and Deborah, a couple they often got together with for dinner and drinks.

"It's okay. We don't need much time," Daron said.

He hoped him caressing her in just the right places would get her hot enough to change her mind, but Linda grabbed his hands and quickly pushed them away from her waist. She turned around and coldly pecked Daron on the lips, then continued primping.

"Babe, you know we can't be late. We have reservations. Besides, my makeup is already done."

Len Richelle

Already aroused, Daron stood there for a few seconds as both his manhood and ego shriveled up to virtually nothing. He turned around and headed towards his closet to finish getting dressed. Grabbing his shoes and suit jacket, he barely looked up as he walked down the hall.

"I'll wait in the car," he mumbled as he headed down the stairs.

Linda was probably one of the most beautiful women on campus when she and Daron met almost twenty years ago. She was very intelligent, too. If it weren't for her, Daron wouldn't have passed his Economics class. They began dating casually in their senior year. Then she went to grad school, while Daron got his first job working in the insurance business. Linda's parents were well off and had very high expectations for her and whoever would be in her life. That put a lot of pressure on Daron, and on the night her father sat down to have a man-to-man talk with him, he wanted to know what plans Daron had for the future and if it was enough to continue with his daughter.

"I'm currently working for an insurance company, sir, and once I learn all aspects of the business, I plan to open my agency."

Daron hadn't thought about it before. He hadn't even thought about what his intentions were with Linda. Her father raised his eyebrows as if he approved of his goals, then nodded his head and wished him the best.

Linda was ecstatic to know her father approved of Daron and added that he was under the impression they'd be marrying soon. That's when the pressure started. Daron suddenly had to figure out how he would open his own business, marry Linda, and provide for her the way she was accustomed to.

In the next nine months, he began working very closely with his boss, asking him a hundred questions a day about insurance. He worked on a small salary but with commission and soon became the top salesperson in the agency. Daron quickly obtained his broker's license, and with Linda's support, opened a small office right before they were married. Before she got the position at the university, she helped Daron open his business and stayed long enough until he was able to hire a couple of people to do the job. She eventually began working as an adjunct professor teaching English Literature, then became one of the topmost requested professors there.

Their marriage was everything to Daron. He had a beautiful, intelligent woman by his side who was there when he was down, made him laugh, and satisfied his sexual needs at the drop of a dime. When he thought they were ready to have children, Linda began to dabble with writing. First, there were a few short stories she had published. Then she took a chance on writing a novel that, although it never made the bestseller's list, gave her enough confidence to pursue her dream of writing. She realized her talent and decided writing was her passion.

"Honey, I think maybe we should hold out on starting a family for a while. I want to take on this writing full-time," she said one day. "I could do special lectures at the university to have something to fall back on, but I really want to try this."

She had his support, and Linda soon adopted the pen name Lauren Lash. She devoted herself to being an author full-time. A sequel followed the first book, then a third and fourth book. Daron was proud of his wife, but the more successful she became, the more distance came between them. Lately, Daron noticed their sex life diminishing. Either Linda was too busy working on one of her books or speeches, or she was too busy preparing for her next trip. Daron tried being romantic, having candlelight dinners, bubble baths, and anything else he could think of to seduce his wife but to no avail. The Linda he knew before her bestsellers had no problem pleasing him in the bedroom. *Ha! In the bedroom, living room, kitchen, car, wherever.* Daron chuckled inside as he reminisced about those days. He imagined that was why he was so drawn to Adrienne.

Len Richelle

She looked like a younger version of Linda and had the same fun, loving personality Linda had so long ago.

Daron sat behind the wheel of his Mercedes and waited for Linda to come down. He slouched in his seat as his imagination took him to the way things used to be. In a quick flash, a vision of Adrienne popped into his head. *She's cute, a bit young.* He had a slight grin on his face as he remembered how sweet she was during her interview. She smiled while sitting across from him and didn't bat an eye as she listened attentively about his company's history. *If only Linda could be so interested.*

"Okay, I'm ready," said Linda.

The sound of her voice startled him as she opened the car door and got in. Feeling a bit guilty for thinking about Adrienne, he quickly started the car and turned on the radio.

Chapter Four

Magnetic Attraction

Only a few weeks after starting her new job, Adrienne believed Daron had a crush on her, as well. At first, she thought it was just her imagination. *Maybe I'm thinking too much into it.* However, whenever Daron passed by her desk, he would give her the biggest smile before turning the corner to go to his office down the hall. He didn't smile the same way with the other women he passed, and if Adrienne wasn't looking up at that moment, he softly spoke her name to get her attention.

It was obvious he had some interest in her, and she enjoyed every bit of his attention. She confirmed his interest when they had their first encounter behind closed doors. Adrienne was working on a hard-to-please client's account. Complaining about the terms in his policy, the client was becoming irate. Not wanting him to feel dissatisfied, Adrienne offered to have a supervisor call him back to help resolve his issue. She looked for Paula, who oversaw customer service matters, but couldn't find her. So, she decided to walk down to Daron's office and tap on his door. When he looked up from his computer, he grinned and motioned for her to come in.

"I'm sorry to disturb you, but I couldn't find Paula, and I wanted to make sure this was taken care of as quickly as possible," said Adrienne as she opened the client's file to show him.

"No problem," he said. "I've got time for you."

Daron sat there displaying his usual cool, sexy smile while adjusting his burgundy and gray striped silk tie and leaning back in his chair. Adrienne caught a whiff of the familiar scent of his cologne—the one she favored—and began experiencing that tingly sensation again. Suddenly, a flashback of her fantasy came to mind. She thought of the dangling pendant between her breasts but was too scared to re-enact the scene. For the next ten minutes, she stumbled through trying to explain her customer's dilemma while trying hard not to lose herself in her thoughts about Daron. Luckily, he acted as if he hadn't noticed her uneasiness and coolly took over the conversation.

"Don't worry, I will handle Mr. Matthews," he assured her.

She handed him the file, and as he reached for it, his fingers gently brushed over hers. The electrifying touch sent chills through Adrienne and made her shiver. He slowly pulled the file from her hand while looking into her eyes. They continued to stare at each other for the next few seconds, and all Adrienne could do was wonder if they were sharing the same forbidden thoughts. Suddenly, the blaring ringing of Daron's phone startled them both and interrupted the moment. That was Adrienne's cue to head back to her desk.

"Thank you, Daron," Adrienne said before turning to leave his office.

She practically floated down the hallway to her cubicle. Daron was everything she fantasized about to be the perfect man for her. Yes, he was much older than anyone she had ever dated, but the moment their eyes met, she instantly felt a connection and was sure it was a sign for something great to happen between them. As she sat at her desk, she imagined the two of them together.

He'll ask me to stay late to work on a project for him, and I'll work hard, coming up with a plan that will improve his business even more. He'll be so impressed with me that at the end of the evening, he will offer to take me out to dinner to celebrate. We'll sip on champagne, and being a little tipsy, I will fall into his arms. Then, while he's looking into my eyes, we will have our first kiss. When I come to work the next day, he will call me into his office to tell me the previous night was everything to him, and he wants to see me again. "What about your wife?" I'll ask him, and he'll reply, "Forget about my wife. You're so much more than she could ever be."

"Uh, you might want to answer that call," said Phyllis.

The light taps on Adrienne's shoulder startled her. Lost in her fantasy, she didn't hear the phone. It was a strict rule to answer all customer service calls on the first ring. By the time she connected the call, the caller had already hung up. Phyllis scrunched her face and shook her head as she turned back to her computer screen.

*****

"Well, it's nice of you to make time for us finally," said Jacki.

She and Staci were already indulging in the bread and olive oil placed on the table and sipping their drinks. Adrienne had been home from college for two weeks before linking up with her best friends.

"Sorry, ladies, been busy with the new job."

Adrienne leaned over and hugged her two friends who she had known since elementary school. Growing up, they lived on the same street, and although Staci and Jacki were several years older than Adrienne, they maintained a close sisterly relationship.

"So, what's up with the job? Any potential boyfriends?"

Jacki asked.

Staci immediately darted a side-eyed glance at Jacki. If she were seated close enough, she would have jabbed her in the rib with her elbow.

"Well, I don't know yet. I just got there, Jacki."

"I'm just saying. You should be having fun this summer, not just working. When you do find somebody, I want us to all go out on a date together. I want you to meet Roderick."

"Jacki, stop," Staci said sternly.

"Staci, what's the problem?" Adrienne snapped, glaring at Staci with fire in her eyes. It was an unspoken reminder for Staci to stay in her place.

For a moment, there was an awkward pause. Adrienne knew where Staci was going with her warning to Jacki, which made her embarrassed and angry.

"I'm sorry," said Staci.

To change the mood, Adrienne shifted in her chair, turned to Jacki, and in a cheery voice, she asked, "So, who is this, Roderick? Someone new? What happened to…Steven?"

"Girl, Steven is about three boyfriends ago. You know I don't keep 'em long if they don't act right!"

The three ladies laughed. Adrienne knew Jacki's track record when it came to men. If she stayed with them for three months, that was a long time for her. Jacki was a single mom with two children but never skipped a beat when it came to dating someone.

"Well, I do have someone I'm interested in," added Adrienne bashfully.

She desperately wanted to tell her girls about her new boss but hesitated. *What good would it do? It's not like I stand a chance. Besides, Staci, with her high morals, would only lecture me.*

"Really? Who?" asked Staci, setting down her glass of water and leaning in.

Staci, married to a doctor, was always skeptical about

anyone Adrienne liked. Adrienne hadn't dated anyone since her last relationship, which ended badly, and Staci would be on her case if she found out Daron was married. *I'll hold off on the details for now.*

"It's new, so I'd rather not say just yet."

"Well, make sure we meet him before you go back to school," said Jacki as she sipped her drink.

Staci rolled her eyes at Jacki's sarcastic response.

"Well, please, just be careful," Staci said.

She gently touched Adrienne's wrist and looked into her eyes. Adrienne knew what she meant; her best friend still didn't trust her.

"And if you need any advice, I'd be happy to talk," Staci added, remembering the way Adrienne's last relationship ended.

They all did.

Chapter Five

So Close, Yet So Far

It wasn't long before Adrienne settled into a routine in her summer job. She endured the bus ride to New Rochelle every day and was always at least fifteen minutes early. Despite her initial fumbling with Phyllis during her first day of training, Adrienne was a fast learner and quickly picked up a clear understanding of her position. She was organized, detail-oriented, and quick to assist others when caught up with her work. Phyllis, who worked in the cubicle next to her, often commented to Paula about how impressed she was with Adrienne's work.

Nonetheless, Adrienne barely made any new friends and still found herself quietly sitting at the table with the ladies during lunchtime, waiting for the right time to fit into the conversation. After several weeks, she gave up on finding things in common to talk about with them. As the women ranted and raved about the latest things their children or grandchildren were doing or some other topic Adrienne had no interest in, she found herself tuning out completely. Daron was the only one with whom she had anything interesting to talk about. He was the only one who appreciated her conversation. Whether it was about her night out with the girls or something as simple as her day doing laundry, Daron wanted to hear about it. And other than the occasional phone call or Paula interrupting for something she felt was urgent, Daron gave Adrienne his full attention. He made her feel significant and purposeful, and if she had a choice, she would choose to share her boring stories about trips to the mall with him any day than sit awkwardly at lunch with women who never even noticed her.

At first, it seemed like their conversations were just small talk. Daron would call her extension and ask for a specific file to review, and they would sit in his office as he looked it over. There would be a question or two regarding the account, but it almost always led to other topics. It wasn't long before he stopped bothering to look through the file and just jumped right into a conversation about something other than work.

"How was your weekend?" he would ask, tossing the unopened file on top of his desk.

Leaning back in his chair with his hands clasped behind his head, he waited for the boring details about the lackluster errands and chores Adrienne did. He listened attentively with eyebrows raised and entirely focused as she described the humdrum events. On occasion, she would mention Staci and Jacki. She would tell him about their weekend antics that typically consisted of having dinner and drinks and Jacki getting a little too tipsy. Daron seemed to have a genuine concern for Adrienne's family and friends, even though he hadn't met them.

"Did your mom get the A/C in her car fixed?" he asked one day.

It thrilled Adrienne to see how much attention he paid to the things happening in her life.

"Yes. She had it repaired over the weekend," Adrienne replied.

"Good, because this week is going to be a scorcher," he said.

They would sometimes spend forty-five minutes to an hour talking about anything other than work. The two would get comfortable chatting as if neither had work to do. Adrienne couldn't wait for their daily talks; he always cared about what she had to say.

Adrienne was certain Daron cared for her in more than a friendly way, and as she gained confidence, she began to find ways to appeal to him even more. For instance, whenever he called her into his office, she always unfastened one more button on her blouse before sauntering into the room. When she sat down, she crossed her legs in her short skirt to expose the top of her thighs. She occasionally caressed her leg with her fingertips and watched as Daron's eyes slowly drifted down in that direction. Adrienne wanted more than their daily talks; she looked forward to taking things to the next level.

It didn't take long before Paula noticed that Adrienne spent significant amounts of time talking to Daron. One afternoon, Daron and Adrienne were in his office laughing and joking. Adrienne nearly fell off her chair while laughing. His sense of humor made him that much more attractive to her.

"I'd better get back out there," she said.

She laughed so hard that she had to catch her breath and wipe the tears from her eyes before walking back to her desk. Paula was standing in the hallway, arms folded and with a look like she was ready to kill. As Adrienne slowly approached her, Paula pulled her to the side.

"I don't want you bothering the CEO of the company with your client issues. If you have any problems with your work, you need to address them with me," she said in the harshest tone.

It was apparent Paula was furious. Adrienne, frightened by Paula's threatening eyes, was practically pinned against the wall as Paula pointed her skinny, crooked finger in her face.

Len Richelle

Paula had been around long enough to know this was how affairs started. Adrienne was too young to see that having a workplace affair could ruin her potential career. If her stern warning to Adrienne would stop what she could see coming, she would do it again.

Paula reminded Adrienne of an old-school teacher from her Catholic school days—stern, mean-looking, and ready to reprimand with a yardstick. Everyone knew she took her work seriously and ran a tight ship, and while at times she could be charming, the staff knew not to cross her. Sometimes it seemed like she had some type of power over Daron, although he owned the company.

After giving her warning, Paula brushed her hands along the sides of her skirt, lifted her chin, and proceeded down the hall wearing a fake smile as if nothing had happened. With her knees shaking and feeling extremely embarrassed, Adrienne crept down the hall to her cubicle, hoping no one witnessed the humiliating confrontation. She had just been banned from Daron's office and suddenly felt alone. Adrienne sat down in her chair to gather her thoughts. *What just happened?* She felt like running back to Daron's office to tell him about the confrontation but was shaking too bad. She needed a moment to calm herself down. *He'll straighten her out. Just wait 'til I talk to him.*

She sat for a few minutes, and just when she began to feel better, Paula came walking towards her. She still had an angry look on her face as she approached Adrienne's desk. Adrienne braced herself for whatever Paula was about to say. However, Paula kept walking by and headed straight towards Daron's office. She could only imagine what Paula would say about her in there.

Over the next couple of days, Adrienne tried to be as low-key as possible. She avoided eye contact with Paula and barely looked up whenever Daron passed through the department. Fearful of Paula and perhaps losing her job, Adrienne did exactly what Paula ordered her to do. She avoided Daron's office like the plague.

"Hey there, Adrienne. Can you please come in with the file we spoke about the other day?"

It was the first time since the confrontation that Daron contacted Adrienne.

"Sure," she responded apprehensively. She hung up her phone and glanced around to make sure Paula was nowhere in sight.

Of course, she was thrilled to hear from Daron, but she still feared the repercussions of disobeying Paula's orders. Nonetheless, she decided this was the opportunity to talk to him. Adrienne walked over to the file cabinet, pulled the file, and slammed the file door. As soon as she turned around, she found herself face to face with an angry-looking Paula, her arms folded across her chest.

"Is that for Mr. Weathers?" Paula asked.

"Y-yes," Adrienne responded.

Paula unfolded her arms and held out her hand. Adrienne slowly handed over the file.

It was too much for Adrienne. Feeling humiliated again, she quickly walked to the nearest restroom and locked herself in a stall, where she bawled her eyes out. After about ten minutes, she dried her eyes and returned to her desk.

She just knew Daron would come to her rescue. Instead, things only got worse. Paula began giving her piles of paperwork to sort through and file. It kept her from dealing with any customers because she was always busy in another section of the office. When she did get to sit at her desk, she noticed Daron was no longer calling for her. He still greeted her with his bright smile in the mornings; however, as soon as he went to his office, Paula would dump another pile of papers on Adrienne's desk.

It's over, she thought. It seemed as if Daron was purposely keeping his distance—perhaps taking orders from Paula.

Len Richelle

Adrienne was devastated.

*****

"Girl, what you do? Got yourself in trouble?" asked Phyllis.

It had been several days since the confrontation with Paula. Adrienne only returned to her desk to gather the rest of the paperwork Paula left for her to file.

"Uh, no. Just doing some extra stuff for Paula."

"Oh, I was wondering because Paula keeps giving me some of your work. And you know your phone is forwarded to her desk, right?"

"Huh?" Adrienne sat in disbelief.

Not only had she not gotten any phone calls from Daron lately, but she realized there were no calls from anyone.

"How do you know?" asked Adrienne.

"Chile, she came here early the other morning. You know I'm here by seven o'clock. I see everything. I saw her dial that code to forward calls. I meant to mention it to you earlier, but that's really none of my business."

"Thank you," Adrienne responded, now on a mission.

Chapter Six

I Run This Company!

Daron's week already started off wrong. Linda surprised him with another last-minute trip, and an argument ensued between them on the evening before she left. Frustrated and annoyed, he came in late to work the next day. Just like the past few days, he wasn't in the best of moods, so he avoided the small talk around the office as he walked past his employees.

After grabbing a cup of coffee from the breakroom, he sat in his office and stewed. He needed to take his mind off the previous night, or else he would be no good for his business.

Adrienne's always good for my mood.

He thought about Adrienne and their afternoon talks. It had become a routine, and he looked forward to seeing her. He saw her as a bright girl, and although she was a bit naïve, she always gave him positive vibes. She had a great sense of humor and made him laugh even on his worst days. He didn't want to admit it, but he was beginning to find her attractive in a more than friendly way. *She's pretty sexy. What the hell.*

He dialed her extension and perked up as he anticipated the sound of her voice.

"Yes, Daron."

"Uh… Oh, hi, Paula."

"Hello. Do you need anything?"

"I-I thought I dialed Adrienne's extension. She was doing some work for me."

"Oh, can I get you anything? I have her working on something right now. You know, the expansion project? She's doing well with it. Moving on up!"

"Oh…great, great. When she gets a chance, please have her bring me the Anderson paperwork. Thanks."

There was a short pause before Paula responded, "Yes, I'll send her over when she's done."

Daron thought it to be strange that Adrienne was working on something new. Paula hadn't mentioned she was considering her for the work, and Daron didn't recall making any plans to start the project. He wanted to wait until the end of summer.

Daron was anxious to see her. Truth was, he needed Adrienne to pull him out of his funk.

He spent the afternoon swiveling around in his chair and staring out the window. He kept looking at his watch and wondered how long Adrienne would be. As he stared out at the courtyard, he admired the garden's flowers. The landscaping of the courtyard was Linda's idea. She suggested giving the staff a place to feel relaxed when they took their breaks during the day. Many of the plants and flowers were the same kind planted in their yard.

After a couple of hours, he heard a light tap on the door. With a huge smile, he swung the chair around, only to be met by a stern-looking Paula standing over his desk and holding the files in her arms. The smile on his face quickly changed to a look of disappointment. He straightened up in his chair as she dropped the files on top of his desk.

"What's this?" he asked.

"These are the accounts you requested. They're from Adrienne." As if she could read Daron's mind, she answered his question. "She's busy right now."

Paula towered over the desk with her arms folded and a look on her face that said she dared him to ask any further questions. Daron hesitated before speaking. He didn't want to seem overly interested in Adrienne, yet he wasn't going to let Paula dictate what was going on in *his* company.

"Thank you," he said, picking up one of the files.

When Paula left the office, Daron tossed the file on his desk. He had no interest in looking at it. It was Adrienne who he wanted to see.

He had no clue about the conversation between Paula and Adrienne, and he couldn't imagine what Adrienne could be doing that made her too busy to see him. *I thought she looked forward to our afternoon talks.* He picked up the phone and dialed Adrienne's extension. Again, Paula answered.

"Uh, I must have dialed the wrong—"

"Is there something I can help you with?"

The annoyed tone in Paula's voice told Daron something was up. *Was Adrienne's extension forwarded to Paula's line?* He was too embarrassed to ask of Adrienne's whereabouts. He wasn't doing anything wrong, but Paula seemed to be trying to control things. *Who does she think she is? I run this company.*

"No, never mind. I'll figure it out."

The next day, Daron decided he would get to the bottom of it. He would wait until lunchtime when most of the staff were out, particularly Paula. He'd check the courtyard and other areas and hopefully catch Adrienne somewhere alone.

At noon, he took a casual walk around the office. As he approached the Customer Service area, he saw the top of her head peeking out from her cubicle. A warm feeling of relief came over him, and he could barely contain his sheepish smile. He quickly glanced around the room to make sure they were alone.

"There you are! How've you been?"

Her plan worked perfectly. Adrienne sat at her desk, slowly

nibbling on her sandwich, hoping Daron would walk through. The timing couldn't have been better. The office was nearly empty.

"Well, you know, I've been busy."

As excited as she was to see him, she knew she had very little time to talk to him before anyone walked in.

"Yeah, Paula told me she's got you on a special assignment. Congratulations! She's moving you on up!"

Adrienne scanned the room before speaking in a low voice.

"I'm not sure it's a way of moving up. I think she's punishing me."

Daron looked confused. "She told me it was a special assignment. Aren't you working on a new project for the company's expansion? Every time I tried to call you, she would pick up because you've been working so hard."

"Is that what she said?"

Adrienne's anger gave her more courage to speak up. She knew she better hurry up and speak before Paula or anyone else came back from lunch.

"Why? What's up?"

Adrienne took a deep breath and exhaled.

"The last time I left your office, she pinned me up against the wall and threatened me, telling me to never go into your office again."

"I thought... Wait, what? What the—"

"She humiliated me in front of everyone in the office. She took away my customer list and stuck me in the dusty closet sorting papers from the shred pile. She even forwarded my calls to make sure you or anyone else couldn't reach me."

Adrienne glanced at her cell phone, then quickly shifted her gaze back to Daron. She did her best to squeeze out a tear, ready to continue convincing Daron of her treatment. She had a closet full of lies if it would bring her closer to Daron.

A moment of silence filled the air between them. Daron stood in disbelief, and then his facial expression turned to one of relief. The truth was, he missed talking to Adrienne and was a little suspicious about this so-called project.

*****

"Paula, what's going on? I didn't authorize you to take away Adrienne's customer list and stick her inside a closet to work. That's not how we treat our employees around here."

Paula sat at the edge of her chair in front of Daron's desk. It was rare for her to be called into his office to be reprimanded.

"I understand, but I was just trying to—"

Daron interrupted. "I don't give a damn what you think you were trying to do." His nostrils flared, and he stood up and leaned across his desk. "You do what I tell you to do, and that's it. Am I clear?"

The nerve of this woman trying to control my business.

Paula's eyes quickly focused on the floor. It embarrassed her to be scolded by Daron. He was almost like a son to her, and they had known each other for so long. She was only trying to protect him from getting himself into something dangerous.

"Yes, sir," she responded, then stood up, turned around, and opened the door to leave.

"And tell Ms. Madison I would like to see her immediately."

Adrienne had been sitting at her desk for almost an hour, doodling on a legal pad. She nervously waited for what would happen next. After her conversation with Daron, he stormed back to his office and closed the door. Staff was returning from their lunch breaks, which meant Paula would be returning soon, as well.

Suddenly, she heard Daron's office door slam and saw Paula coming from that direction. She had an angry look in her eyes as she charged directly towards Adrienne's desk. Adrienne sat straight up in her chair and braced herself. When she reached Adrienne's desk, Paula bent over closely and whispered in her ear.

"Mr. Weathers would like to see you in his office. *Now*."

Adrienne could feel the warmth of Paula's breath as she emphasized the word *now*. When Paula straightened up, her face revealed a soft, pleasant smile as she began walking back towards her office. A few seconds later, Adrienne heard Paula's door slam shut.

Adrienne hesitated before getting out of her seat. She first looked around to see if anyone else noticed Paula approaching her. Adrienne could hear Phyllis, who was sitting in the cubicle next to her, talking on the phone to a customer. She peeked around the divider to find Phyllis leaned over and focused on the computer screen. She was too deep into the conversation to have noticed. In the background, she heard the clicking of computer keys and other representatives talking on the phone to their customers or each other. No one appeared to have been watching her interaction with Paula. Once she was confident about that, Adrienne stood up and cautiously walked down the hall. She knew Daron liked her, but she wasn't sure what transpired between the two about her. It was time to confront her fate.

Daron was in his office with the door closed. Through the door's glass, Adrienne could see him staring at his computer screen with his hands together under his chin—almost as if praying. She gently knocked, and after looking up, he motioned for her to enter. She apprehensively walked in and stood by the door until he gestured for her to sit down. He appeared very relaxed and not as serious as she expected him to be, especially after Paula's angry door slamming.

He closed the planner sitting in front of him, clasped his hands atop his desk, and took a deep breath. The white gold wedding band with diamonds glistened sharply in her eyes.

"I'll get straight to it," he said. "I wanted to let you know that you do *not* have to go through Paula if I request any information from you. If you have issues with any clients or any of the work, report straight to me."

He looked her in the eye and waited for a response. Adrienne looked back at him but said nothing. He cleared his throat and leaned in closer before speaking again.

"I am here if you need anything."

Adrienne looked up, and their eyes met for what seemed like an eternity. She had no idea what he and Paula discussed but could only imagine she got the verbal ass-whooping she deserved. It excited her to know that she now had carte blanche with the boss. She missed their daily talks, and in her opinion, there was nothing wrong with what they were doing. At least, that's what she was telling herself. However, Adrienne had feelings for Daron, and she was sure he was starting to feel the same way. She shook those thoughts from her head. They knew their limits. They could admire each other and even flirt if they never crossed that line. As long as she was clear about those things, she would be fine.

Daron must have realized how long the two had been gazing at each other because he cleared his throat and blushed with embarrassment. Adrienne stood up to leave, and as she thanked him, Daron waved for her to sit back down.

"Relax. We have a lot of catching up to do. What's up for the weekend?"

Chapter Seven
Paula's Last Laugh

By the end of the summer, Adrienne realized she was in love with Daron. She no longer cared that he was married; his wife was his problem, not hers. She started arriving to work earlier so she wouldn't miss him passing by her desk when coming in. That way, she would get a whiff of his cologne and see his gorgeous smile as he greeted her with "Good morning, Adrienne," every day. She'd check out his custom-tailored suit from head to toe and admire how he color-coordinated his ties, shirts, and watches. Then she stared as he continued down the hall to his office until he was out of her sight. After lunch, she would either get an email or a phone call from him requesting to see her in his office. They would spend time talking and laughing, and best of all, Paula never said a word, although Adrienne sensed she was fuming inside. It didn't matter. Adrienne was floating on a cloud at work; at home, everyone else seemed to notice, as well.

Adrienne wanted to do something special for Daron. She thought their *relationship* had escalated to the next level. She loved him and wanted him to know it. Adrienne had taken her hard-earned money and went shopping that weekend. She found a tie pin she thought would look good.

That Monday morning, she arrived early before most of her co-workers. Daron was in his office. She knocked softly at the door. When he saw it was her, he immediately started grinning. Adrienne was nervous, thinking he may not like her gesture. As she approached his desk, she pulled the small gift-wrapped box from behind her back and set it on the desk in front of him. Surprise registered on his face, and his smile grew bigger. Adrienne explained the gift as a small trinket she thought he might like. Daron told her that he loved it. The tie pin was gold with his initials on it.

Daron put the pin on, thanking Adrienne profusely and telling her that she shouldn't have spent her money on him. Daron knew it was inappropriate to accept Adrienne's gift, but it was more than his wife had done for him in months. It made him feel good. So, yeah, he accepted it. Daron wanted to plant the wettest kiss on Adrienne's lips but knew he couldn't, so he remained seated.

Adrienne was elated that Daron loved his gift. He loved her; she could see that so clearly now. No, he hadn't said it, but she felt it just the same. Adrienne left Daron's office floating on cloud nine. She continued smiling for the whole day, and Paula, with her watchful eye, couldn't do anything about what had transpired between Adrienne and Daron.

*****

"So, how's the job coming along?" asked Jacki.

Adrienne stopped by her house one evening after work. They hadn't seen each other in a few weeks and wanted to catch up on everything going on in each other's lives. They were sharing a plate of nachos, and Jacki had made a batch of frozen margaritas.

"It's great, but summer is going by so fast. It's almost time for me to go back to school."

The alcohol was starting to enhance Adrienne's emotional state, and she was beginning to miss Daron already.

"Well, what's going on? Didn't you say you met someone there?" Jacki asked.

"Yes, and I think we're in love," she blurted out, then realized she may have had one too many margaritas.

"What? In love?" Jacki put her drink down and leaned in closer to Adrienne.

Adrienne had no idea why she said what she did. However, once she heard her own words, she started feeling good about it. She liked the idea of her and Daron being in love. Although nothing close to that had been mentioned between the two, Adrienne had high hopes that someday, somehow, her dreams would come true.

"Well, it's just the beginning stages of the relationship. I didn't want to get serious since I'm going back to school."

"You've got to tell me all about him. Does Staci know? Am I the last to know?" Looking frustrated, Jacki sat closer to her and waited for an explanation.

"You aren't the last to know. You know more than anyone so far. We're keeping things quiet—at least until I come back next year."

Adrienne figured if she downplayed it, Jacki would back off, and it worked. She took another sip of her margarita and quickly changed the subject.

"Just make sure you don't leave me out of anything new that happens. Want another margarita?"

Adrienne quickly responded yes. Anything to get off the subject.

*****

It was the last week of work before going back to school. Adrienne was anxious to return to school yet sad about leaving Daron. They had developed a close friendship, and she wasn't sure how things would end.

"When is your last day again?" he asked.

They were having one of their one-on-one discussions that afternoon, and she casually mentioned having to pack for her return to Connecticut.

"Two weeks from today," she answered.

"Well, we'll have to make sure we send you off with something nice," Daron said, then scribbled something inside his planner before closing it.

"Oh, you don't have to do anything special," she said.

Adrienne blushed, knowing Daron wanted to do something nice for her. However, what she imagined for her going away party did not include everyone else in the office. She would have preferred to have a private send-off with Daron alone.

I'd rather it just be you and me. Pick me up in that Mercedes and take me to one of those fancy restaurants you talk about. Spend the evening with me over a candlelight dinner, then whisper in my ear that you love me. Just like I love you. We'll go back to your place and—

"Hello? Earth to Adrienne?"

Adrienne snapped out of her trance as Daron tried to get her attention.

"I'm sorry. What did you say? I-I was thinking about all the things I need to do before I leave."

Daron chuckled and shook his head. "College days. I remember them well. I was saying that I'm going to make *sure* we do something nice for you before you leave. Okay?"

*****

At the end of the week, Paula approached her, and to Adrienne's surprise, she learned that Paula was the one coordinating her going away party.

"Is there anything special you would like for your party?" she asked, holding a pen and pad ready to take notes.

"I like Italian food," Adrienne responded with a smile. "Maybe chocolate cake?"

Paula nodded and scribbled down Adrienne's requests, then gave her a warm smile. It wasn't a phony smile like she usually gave her. Adrienne assumed she was happy to see her finally leaving.

*****

On her last day of work, Adrienne wore a white blouse with sheer long sleeves and a turquoise skirt with matching stilettos. She had doubts that Daron would take her out to say goodbye, but she fantasized all day it would happen. After all, they had become close; surely, he would want to have one last special moment with her.

She spent the morning emptying her workstation and sending emails to some of the clients, thanking them for working with her and wishing them well. She noticed Daron had not passed by her desk all morning. He knew this was her last day, and he insisted on giving her a going away party. She assured herself that he would be there in time. *Not unless he is saving his goodbye for later.* She giggled to herself at her unforbidden thoughts.

The morning went by quickly, and by noon, an aroma of delicious Italian food was in the air.

"Lunch is ready in the courtyard," announced Paula as she approached her desk. "Come join us. It's your day!"

She had that same sweet smile as she did earlier in the week, and while Adrienne was somewhat skeptical, she dismissed Paula's unusual kindness and looked forward to her going away luncheon.

Adrienne quickly applied a coat of lipstick and ran her fingers through her hair. She wanted to look good for the pictures she and Daron would take as he stood before the rest of the staff while expressing his best wishes to Adrienne. She was sure Daron had bought her an expensive gift; she knew he would want to reciprocate what she had done for him. Excited, she could hardly contain herself. *Where is Daron anyway?* Adrienne took a glimpse of herself in one of the mirrored glass windows as she followed Paula down the hall. *He'll love me in this turquoise skirt.*

As they passed his office, she noticed Daron's office lights were off. She assumed he was already waiting for her in the courtyard with everyone else. She imagined his handsome smile as she made her grand entrance. They continued down the hall, Paula quickly walking ahead of her while occasionally turning to look back with a smile. When they stepped out into the courtyard, it seemed like everyone from the office was there waiting for her. Streamers and balloons hung from tree branches, and brightly colored tablecloths and centerpieces decorated the tables. Alongside one wall were long tables covered with trays of delicious pasta dishes, salads, and chocolate cake. Next to that table was a smaller table with several cards and gifts. Everyone clapped as she walked in, and she was grateful for the warmth and love.

After thanking everyone for the warm reception, Adrienne looked around the courtyard for Daron. He was nowhere in sight, but Adrienne assumed he would show up any minute to give his speech and let everyone know how much he appreciated her.

Paula walked over and stood in front of the crowd to get everyone's attention. When everyone quieted down, she turned to Adrienne and gently placed her left hand on her shoulder.

"Adrienne, on behalf of Mr. Weathers and the entire company, we would like to express our sincere appreciation for working with us this summer. Unfortunately, Mr. Weathers could not be here this afternoon due to a scheduling conflict, but he would like you to know how much of an asset you've been for the company, and he wishes you the best in your senior college year."

Adrienne couldn't believe what she had heard. *What?!?* As the crowd applauded, Adrienne put on a fake smile while fighting back her tears. She was devastated. *What did I just hear?* Still unable to comprehend why Daron was not there for her, she nodded her head and thanked everyone. *What scheduling conflict could he possibly have on this day?*

After the applauding died down, Phyllis and a couple of the ladies from her department wished her well. They said some very nice things about Adrienne, but she barely heard a word. All she could do was focus on Daron and nod her head, pretending to listen. When Paula announced it was time to eat, the crowd quickly dispersed and lined up at the buffet table, leaving Adrienne standing alone and confused.

After finally helping herself to a small plate of pasta, she sat at one of the tables with some of the ladies she usually sat with for lunch. Adrienne barely touched her food as they rambled on about *which pasta dish tasted better, how good Monique's lasagna tasted last week,* and *what bakery the chocolate cake came from.* No one focused on Adrienne, even though the luncheon was because of her. *If Daron were here, all of his attention would be on me, and he would be asking a ton of questions about me going back to school.*

While everyone continued eating, Paula insisted that Adrienne open the gifts and cards. Adrienne couldn't care less about those gifts; she was more concerned about Daron's whereabouts. However, she couldn't let anyone see her disappointment, so she started opening the gifts while pretending to be gracious and excited.

When Paula handed her the last gift, she did so while making deliberate eye contact with Adrienne.

"Here… This is from Mr. Weathers. Again, he apologizes that he couldn't stay to see you off, but he had an important engagement."

Paula winked at Adrienne, and then her sweet smile turned into an evil grin. It was all coming together. *Paula had something to do with Daron not being here.*

"Thank you," Adrienne said as she accepted the neatly wrapped gift from Paula.

Everyone gathered around as she carefully unwrapped the small box. When she unfolded the white tissue paper, it revealed a glass-like statue with the words *THANK YOU FOR YOUR EXCELLENT CUSTOMER SERVICE* and the D.L. Weathers Insurance logo etched underneath.

Adrienne was dumbfounded; it was hardly the kind of gift Adrienne thought Daron would have picked for her. He would have given her something more personal—not a trophy that didn't even have her name on it. Still, she wouldn't dare let Paula see her disappointment. She graciously thanked her and Daron for the lovely gift.

They wrapped up the party around 3:30 p.m. Adrienne packed all the gifts and cards in a large shopping bag, made her rounds through the office one last time, and then walked out the office doors for good. As she stood at the bus stop, she thought about how Paula never liked her, especially after Daron intercepted her attempt to ban Adrienne from talking to him. Paula hated hearing them behind closed doors, loudly laughing and joking every afternoon. She had lain in wait for a chance to get back at Adrienne. Today, she achieved it. Paula had the last laugh.

Chapter Eight

A Sneaky Diversion

It was Thursday evening, and Daron and Linda were entertaining their friends, Macy, one of Linda's sorority sisters, and her husband, Bill, for dinner. As they sat by the pool sipping on glasses of wine, Daron grilled steaks, lobster, and shrimp while Linda boasted with stories portraying a happy marriage.

"We're probably going back to Bora Bora next year. We loved it so much!" claimed Linda. "Why don't you guys join us?"

Linda looked at the couple, who looked at each other. Macy and Bill were not as wealthy as Daron and Linda, and Linda knew it. Daron was becoming annoyed with the entire conversation. Linda was always bragging about something and loved trying to impress others by showing off material things. Although Daron enjoyed all of it as much as Linda, he never wanted to show it off to his friends, especially those whom he knew didn't have as much.

Daron shook his head as he flipped the steaks. He couldn't wait until the evening was over.

After the couple left, Daron cleaned up the patio and took a shower before going to bed. Linda would not stop talking about how impressed her friends were with the evening.

"We showed them what real living is like, huh, hon? I mean, who wouldn't want our life?"

"When are you going to show me the same attention you show these material things?" Daron asked, looking at the back of Linda as she moved around the kitchen, putting things away.

"What did you say, bae?" Linda asked, turning around to look at Daron. Caught up in what she said, she hadn't heard him.

"Nothing," Daron replied with a smirk before leaving the kitchen. As much as he wanted to have this conversation, he had no energy for it.

As Daron lay in bed, his thoughts for Linda were mixed. He loved his wife and missed the closeness they used to have. More and more, it seemed like she cared less for him and more about being in the spotlight and showing off the material things he provided for her.

He turned over on his side and tried to drift off to sleep. As he did, he focused his thoughts on Adrienne. Her last day was tomorrow, and he was going to miss her. Daron had instructed Paula to set everything up and was looking forward to seeing the smile on Adrienne's face.

Throw her a nice party; find out whatever she wants to eat and order it, he had told Paula. *I want her to enjoy herself. Oh, and let's get her a nice gift from the jewelry shop I usually order from.*

Daron soon drifted off to sleep, looking forward to Adrienne's going away party the next day. That is until he was awakened by the ringing of his cell phone two hours later.

"Hi, Daron. It's Paula. Sorry to bother you, but I just wanted to make sure you were aware of the car service picking you up at five a.m."

Daron looked at the phone with confusion. He was half

asleep and not sure he heard Paula clearly.

"I'm sorry, what did you say?"

"Don't you remember?" Paula asked. "You have a brokers' conference in Denver starting tomorrow. Check-in for the conference is by ten a.m. That's why you have such an early flight."

"Oh, no, I can't make that—"

"Do you need me to cancel? It's non-refundable, including the flight. Oh, and you are on the panel to speak. Don't you remember? I typed your talking points for you."

Daron paused for a moment and tried to think things through. *How could I have forgotten?* He vaguely remembered discussing a conference in Colorado, but he didn't remember registering for it nor confirming with Paula that he was going. Adrienne would be so disappointed if he didn't show up, but he knew how important it was to keep his engagements, especially if he was speaking on a panel. After debating in his head, he agreed it was best if he attended. Then he asked Paula to do him a favor and relay a message to Adrienne.

"Please tell her I'm sorry I couldn't make it. Oh, and let her know if she needs a job next summer, don't hesitate to contact me. And can you send me those talking points again? I have no idea where I saved them."

"Of course," Paula replied. "Of course."

Paula couldn't have been more pleased with herself. She would finally be rid of what she considered a bothersome problem—Adrienne. They would never have to see her again.

Chapter Nine

School Daze

"Do you have everything?" Adrienne's mother asked her.

Adrienne was loading the last duffle bag into the trunk of her car. Her mother looked around for something to do besides standing there. She worried about Adrienne. After the disappointing goodbye party at work, Adrienne had fallen into a slump and kept herself locked in her room until yesterday when she began to pack.

"I'm good," she replied.

Adrienne didn't bother to make eye contact. She was hurting too much and afraid she would lose trying to hold back her tears if she looked up.

Kara came running outside acting cheery and energetic. Adrienne always hated her upbeat demeanor.

"I'm gonna miss my big sis," said Kara, wrapping her arms around Adrienne's waist from behind and burying her head in the middle of her back.

Adrienne could have turned around and reciprocated the hug, but she was stubborn and didn't.

She returned to school feeling crushed. Adrienne still had

not gotten over Daron not saying goodbye to her. She was sure Paula purposely arranged some conference for him to attend at the last minute so he would miss the party. Adrienne decided she would bury herself in schoolwork, hoping her studies and the distance between them would help her forget him. However, she started something she found difficult to get out of; she and Daron had become quite popular around campus.

It began the day after her arrival when she met up with a few friends from the old dorm. After everyone settled in, they got together to catch up on things they did over the summer. A couple of the girls shared stories about their summer flings, while others talked about the places they traveled. They went on and on about all their exciting adventures and romances while Adrienne sat quietly, not having anything to share.

Sitting in the dorm room with the girls suddenly reminded her of the times she spent having lunch with the ladies in the courtyard. Everyone talked over one another, going from one exciting experience to the next. Meanwhile, Adrienne hadn't experienced a summer fling or traveled to an exotic island. She only had a summer crush and spent most of the summer trying to keep cool with the help of the ceiling fan in her room. She listened to the girls' sensational stories about their trips to Puerto Rico and Punta Cana with their families or boyfriends; the most exciting thing she did was attend a block party where some b-list old-school rappers performed. She was starting to feel irrelevant again and longed for another conversation with Daron.

At least Daron would appreciate hearing about the old-school block party.

Finally, when one of the girls asked Adrienne about her summer, she had her chance to speak, but what came out of her mouth was the start of many lies that even she began to believe.

"As soon as I graduate, my boyfriend and I are getting engaged."

64

"Oh my God," said Danisha. "Really? Who is he?"

"His name is Daron. He's the CEO of the company I worked for this summer. We fell in love, and before I left to come back to school, he told me that he wanted to marry me. I said yes, but I don't want it to be official until I'm home from college."

"You're going to marry this guy? Didn't you guys just meet over the summer?" asked Andrea, one of her roommates.

It was too late to take it back, so she felt compelled to stick with her story. Then, after some thought, the story started sounding good to her.

"Yes. We fell in love quickly. Soon after he hired me, he promoted me to be his office manager. I replaced the last office manager because she was doing a lousy job."

A vision of Paula and her long, skinny fingers pointing at her came to her mind.

The girls were in awe of her summer love story. They asked more questions about Daron and Adrienne. *Is he good-looking? What does your mother think of him? Will you have a big wedding?* She kept her answers simple: *Yes. She loves him. Probably not.* Adrienne hadn't had time to sort out the details, and if she were going to continue with her make-believe story, she would have to come up with something great. So far, no one else's summer story compared to hers. She told them about the concerts, the baseball games, and the weekend getaways— all the things Daron had done with his wife. The girls practically drooled with envy, and finally, she was the center of attention.

After her fifteen minutes of storytelling, the girls returned to their assigned dorm rooms, and a tinge of guilt suddenly came over her. She had a habit of lying, but having never lied like this before, she tried to justify her reasons for doing so. Had she told the truth about her summer, she would have looked like the loneliest senior in the dorm.

Besides, after this year, I'll never see any of these girls again.

She reminded herself that she would have to mention Daron's name from time to time and keep up with her story.

*****

Making it through the school year was more challenging than the previous years. Adrienne could not concentrate with Daron always on her mind. She sometimes called his office, hoping to hear his voice but only to have Paula, who often screened his calls, answer for him. She searched for his cell number online, but it was unlisted, and he had no social media pages except for his company's website.

The website was the closest she could get to being with him, and Adrienne checked it daily. She would visit the website, clicking on the tabs and links to read every detail about his company. She studied the services offered, the types of insurance provided, and looked through the staff directory, reminiscing about her former co-workers and, of course, Daron. She smiled when she read his name in large, bold letters. His bio stated he had been in the insurance business for fifteen years. He graduated from Quinnipiac University, and his website boasted of his company having the latest state-of-the-art programs to ensure the best customer service. She was proud of her man and dreamed of the stories she told about them turning into reality.

A photo of Daron in a business suit was in the left-hand corner of the webpage. Underneath his photo was *Daron Weathers, Broker and CEO*—his name and title.

Every evening before bed, she would brush her fingers over his picture and whisper goodnight. She would trace over the hair on his head, his beautiful, light-brown eyes, and his broad shoulders. She sometimes thought it was silly, but it helped her sleep at night and kept his image in her head.

When school was out for Christmas break, Adrienne couldn't wait to get home to see what Daron was up to. She had already told her roommates all the plans she and Daron made for the holidays. She led everyone to believe she would be having a spectacular time shopping for gifts, spending time with his family, and enjoying the holiday season.

"Maybe he'll give you a ring for Christmas," said Danisha.

"Oh, no. I was adamant that I don't want to make it official until I am home at the end of the school year."

Adrienne didn't want to have to go out and buy a fake engagement ring just yet. She knew her friends would make it a big deal about her engagement, and she thought it was best to just keep them at bay for now.

Not long after arriving home for the holidays, Adrienne was anxious to check on Daron. So, she asked to borrow her mother's car almost immediately.

"Where are you going, Adrienne? You just got home. Spend some time with your family."

"I will, Mom. I just need to do some shopping. Plus, I want to catch up with the girls."

It was easy to convince her mother. After all, why wouldn't Adrienne want to do some Christmas shopping and meet up with her friends? When she took the car early the next morning, she drove straight to New Rochelle to Daron's company even though she knew he wouldn't be there. It was close to Christmas, and this was the time of the year when he went down to the Keys to spend the holidays with his wife, Linda. She remembered Daron telling her about their second home in Key Largo and how Linda usually went down first; then Daron followed her down there for Christmas. *I guess it's a thing wealthy people do*, she thought.

As she pulled into the lot, only a few cars were parked inside. The space where Daron usually parked was empty. That confirmed that he had to be out of town.

Before heading back home, she made one more stop. She put the address in her GPS and followed the directions leading to Scarsdale. Turning onto the private road, she slowed down in front of the enormous Mediterranean home. It was her first time driving past Daron's house, and she gasped at the size of it. It was beautifully decorated with Christmas ornaments, lights, and a massive wreath hanging above the front door. From the looks of the décor, only professionals would have taken the time to put up the lavish ornaments. *It was probably Linda's idea.* She figured only Linda would want to decorate their home so extravagantly, even if they were out of town.

It was more than Adrienne could take. She hadn't seen or heard from Daron in months. Somehow, someway she wanted Daron to know what he meant to her. Adrienne left to find the supplies she would need to leave a little gift from her to Daron.

*****

After studying her work, Adrienne headed back home. She was proud of herself and knew Daron would love her kind gesture. She missed Daron and wondered what he and Linda were doing at that very moment. She had to catch herself as she began imagining herself taking the next flight to Florida. *I could get there by the end of the day.* She laughed at herself. *Only a stalker would do something like that.* But she wasn't a stalker; she was in love, and he loved her. The thoughts of them being together were getting better and better. She had to see Daron, and she couldn't wait. If it were only a glimpse of him from a distance, it would be good enough for her.

When Adrienne arrived back at her mother's house, dinner was ready, but she wasn't hungry. Instead, Adrienne went to her room, opened her laptop, and began her search to locate Mr. and Mrs. Daron Weathers. It didn't take long to find the information that Adrienne sought. Now, to work out the logistics. She would catch a flight in two days, travel to the Keys that morning, and return home later that night. *It'll be tough, but anything's possible.* Adrienne would concoct a story, telling her mother that she was interviewing for a job she didn't want but was going because it was a free trip.

Adrienne's plan was easier to execute than she thought. Her mother didn't ask a lot of questions. Adrienne was glad because she didn't want to keep up with so many lies. She stayed up most of the night before her flight, trying to pick the right outfit even though she didn't plan for Daron to see her. Adrienne left at five in the morning to make her eight o'clock flight. She didn't want to leave anything to chance. This was an expensive endeavor for a college student. Between the cost of the plane ticket, Uber ride, and rental car, it made a huge dent in Adrienne's savings, but she told herself that Daron was worth every penny.

Once the flight landed, Adrienne took a shuttle to pick up her rental. Looking at her watch, it was ten-thirty. She prayed Daron was at home. She entered Daron's address in the GPS, put the car in drive, and pulled off. After about an hour and twenty minutes, Adrienne found herself sitting in front of Daron and Linda's house. She scooted down in the driver's seat as far as she could go. The house looked just like it did on the internet—a well maintained, beachfront property. It all spelled success. Adrienne would encourage Daron to keep this house after his divorce, thinking her mother would love it. Adrienne was sure it was big enough that her mother could have her own space in the place.

After sitting for almost an hour, the front door opened. Linda exited the house first, laughing and looking behind her. Daron came through the doorway laughing, too. Adrienne sat up straight after seeing him. He was breathtaking in all white, wearing a polo shirt with white pants and Nike slides.

"Come here," Daron said to the back of Linda.

She stopped, waiting for Daron. He closed the distance between them, pulling her into his embrace and putting his hands on her ass.

"I love you," he said before dipping his head to kiss his wife passionately.

Len Richelle

This vacation had been what he hoped for—a rekindling of the love he felt for Linda all those years ago. There in Florida, he had her undivided attention. However, things probably would go back to the way they were before coming to Florida, but Daron wouldn't think about it. He would just enjoy his wife.

Tears formed in Adrienne's eyes as she watched this scene play out. She had come to the quick conclusion that Daron was cheating on her with his wife.

She started the car and sped off. She had to get away, or else she might get out of the car and confront Daron. Once she turned down a side street, Adrienne shut off the engine and started crying.

"Why is he still with her?" she asked herself out loud.

She felt betrayed. Truthfully, she had spent the last semester in a make-believe relationship with this man, and by now, it felt real. Adrienne became enraged—hitting the steering wheel with her fists, the back of the car seat with her arms, and beating the dashboard until her hands hurt. Just as quick as she had gone from zero to ten, she calmed down just as quick.

Adrienne looked at herself in the rearview mirror, making the necessary adjustments to her hair, putting herself back together. She smiled at her reflection, conceding that Daron was Linda's husband for now, but she would have Daron for the rest of her life.

Adrienne went to the airport to catch her flight home. She was elated that she had seen Daron. The part where she watched him kiss his wife was a thing of the past—something she erased from her mind.

*****

Daron and Linda returned home from their vacation. The sleek SUV had picked them up at the airport, and when the driver turned onto their street, they found messages written in chalk on the road.

I can't wait to see you.

I miss you terribly.

I love you.

The third message was written right in front of their house.

Linda thought it was the cutest thing she had ever seen, believing the messages were the work of a love-struck teenager. She joked that Daron should have come up with something like that for her. Daron smiled despite the hair standing up on the back of his neck. He could feel there was more to this than Linda thought.

*****

Adrienne barely made it through her senior year because she spent so much time daydreaming in class and was too distracted to take many notes during the lectures. However, she managed to maintain her story about Daron until the end of the year without anyone suspecting it was a lie. She had lied so much that she believed the relationship herself.

The night before graduation, she pretended she had received a phone call from Daron saying he could not make the ceremony.

"His mom is sick," she said to her roommate. "She had to be rushed to the hospital."

As she spoke those words, she asked God for forgiveness. She may have lied many times, but she didn't like lying about anyone's health. Nevertheless, her plan worked because everyone was sympathetic and expressed their concern for Daron's mother.

Adrienne feigned being worried the entire evening, and on graduation day, she relayed the message that her declining health was improving. She didn't want to spend her celebratory day moping around about someone's fake illness.

Adrienne put on her pink-floral dress, nude-colored stiletto

Len Richelle

strap sandals, and gold heart pendant on the morning of graduation. She had printed out Daron's website photo earlier in the week and taped it to the inside of her graduation cap. It was silly, but the only way she could feel close to him without him being there.

Everyone was there to support her for the graduation—Mom, Kara, Jacki, Staci, Uncle Jim and his wife, Pam, and even Adrienne's dad, who surprisingly made the trip without her stepmother, Abby, tagging along.

At the end of the ceremony, Adrienne met everyone near the exit doors by the foot of the stage. Her mother stood holding a beautiful bouquet, and Kara had a bunch of balloons. Both were the first to greet her with big hugs and smiles as Adrienne watched her father patiently waiting off to the side. Uncle Jim and Aunt Pam were standing near her dad and occasionally made small talk with him, while Staci and Jacki took selfies using the crowd as the backdrop. What should have been an exciting day for Adrienne felt empty without Daron. She only imagined him being so proud of her as she strutted across the stage.

He approaches me and kisses me softly on the lips. "Congratulations, baby. I'm so proud of you," he whispers. Then he offers to take everyone into town for a dinner celebration. We all meet up at the most expensive steakhouse, where we enjoy prime rib, lobster mac and cheese, and Crème Brule for dessert. Daron stands up, makes a toast to me, and lets everyone know how special I am to him. Staci and Jacki look at each other with envy in their eyes but try to put on a smile. After dinner, I kiss everyone goodbye, and Daron whisks me off in his Mercedes. He has a special surprise for me, and I spend the road trip trying to guess what it is. We end up at the airport, where we board a private jet heading to Miami. When we land in Miami, a limousine awaits us and drives us to Key Largo, where we spend the weekend at his vacation home.

72

She hadn't given up on the idea that when Daron divorced Linda, they would move into the four-bedroom luxury home with marble floors and the backyard that overlooked a spectacular waterfront view. Adrienne imagined the two of them spending their winters there just as he and Linda did.

During the day, we will make love by the pool and, in the evening, sit on the deck behind the house to take in the breathtaking pink and lavender hues of the sky as the orange sun settles into the coral-blue waters. Sometimes we will drive our electric golf cart into the village for shopping and then stop for lunch at one of the private clubs to enjoy the day's fresh catch.

"Adrienne, go speak to your father," her mother said, nudging her shoulder.

Adrienne snapped out of her trance and turned to the man leaning against the wall. He took pictures of her with his cell phone as she approached.

"Hi, Dad," she said.

He hugged her and held her tightly. Adrienne rarely saw him anymore, and he felt like a stranger to her. She had been avoiding him since the incident. Perhaps she was too embarrassed to face him.

"You're not returning my calls, kiddo," her father said.

She turned her head towards Staci and Jacki taking selfies with her mother and Kara.

"Is everything okay?" he asked while trying to make eye contact with Adrienne.

She finally turned to him.

"Sure, Dad. Everything's okay. How's Abby?"

Although she had no interest in his new wife, it was her attempt at changing the subject.

Her father smiled, patted her on the back, and then looked off into the distant crowd. He wanted to talk to his daughter somewhere quiet. He knew she had been avoiding him and understood why. Yet, he still loved her no matter what, and he wanted to tell his oldest daughter that he would always be there for her. He wanted to make sure she was staying on the right path and not falling back into the old habits. *At least she's a college graduate now. She must be focused if she did that.* He began to say something to her, but Staci and Jacki walked up on both sides of Adrienne and grabbed her arms.

"Congratulations!" they yelled in unison.

Staci handed Adrienne a bouquet of flowers. The three of them stood in a group hug as her father snapped pictures with his cell phone. Adrienne was grateful for the interruption. It wasn't a conversation she was ready to have.

Chapter Ten

The Set-Up

As promised, Adrienne received a used car from her parents as a graduation gift. The burgundy Kia Sportage was just enough for Adrienne to get around, and she was grateful she no longer had to take the bus around town—especially with the mission that she was about to launch soon. After being home from college for two weeks, she was hired by an insurance company across town from Daron's company. She hadn't bothered to try to get a job working for Daron. Paula had already caused too much drama for that. Besides, Adrienne had other things on her agenda for Daron, and working together would only draw attention to the two of them.

The Fredericks Insurance Group was located between a pizza parlor and a shoe repair shop in a strip mall. It was no comparison to Daron's office. D.L. Weather's Insurance was classier and had newer furniture and high-tech equipment. At Fredericks Insurance, Adrienne sat in a small cubicle in the back of the office, and the view outside her window was of an alleyway filled with large trash dumpsters.

Adrienne's new boss, Mr. Fredericks, was an older, portly man, and based on his run-down shoes, his company didn't make nearly as much money as Daron's. There were about fifteen people in the entire office. Already familiar with customer service, Adrienne knew she would have no problem learning her job quickly. That would leave her more time to work on a plan to see Daron again.

After her first week of work, she came home to find her mother and Kara waiting for her. Mom had fixed a pan of lasagna, one of Adrienne's favorite meals, and Kara baked cupcakes.

"What's this for?" she asked.

"It's to celebrate your first week at your new job," answered her mother.

The look in her eyes let Adrienne know how proud she was of how far her daughter had come. Kara smiled as she looked up in awe of her big sister.

They sat down and enjoyed the meal together. Mom wanted to know all the details of her week, and Kara was attentively waiting to hear them, as well. Adrienne gave them the basics about the job, but her mind was focused on Daron. She couldn't help it. Working in the insurance business only reminded her of him. She missed him more than ever, and her urge to see him only grew stronger.

One day after work, she drove across town to Daron's agency. A few cars were still in the parking lot, and she quickly passed through to look for his. She didn't find a Mercedes; however, there was a shiny new black Escalade in Daron's assigned spot. Adrienne was impressed with his new ride and imagined herself in the passenger seat. She made a mental note of the license plate before driving away.

The following week, work was slower than usual. Mr. Fredericks was on vacation, and the other staff hung around the cubicles laughing and chatting. Since it was close to lunchtime, Adrienne thought it would be a good time to take her break.

Again, she drove her car across town to Daron's company. Once she spotted the Escalade, she felt the same tingly feeling she used to feel whenever he passed her desk. She contemplated going inside to the receptionist to ask for him but thought about Paula and decided to spare herself any embarrassment of being turned away.

The next day was a Friday. The alarm clock sounded, and Adrienne lay in bed thinking of Daron. Suddenly, the perfect idea came to mind, and she jumped out of bed to get ready. Once dressed, she called her job to tell them she was having car trouble and would arrive late. Then she called for a Lyft to drive her to the nearest car rental, where she picked up the cheapest vehicle before heading to work. She made sure her outfit was perfect—gold-toned low-cut blouse, black slacks to enhance her curves, and a pair of black heels. After adding the bronze shimmer lipstick, her makeup was just right, and there was not a hair out of place.

Around three o'clock, she used the excuse that she had to pick up her car from the mechanic and headed across town to Daron's company. It was about 3:25 p.m. when she arrived and parked outside the lot's gates. With her sunglasses covering her eyes, she sank low in the seat so she would not be recognized by any staff leaving from work.

Adrienne knew Daron usually left work early on Fridays. However, by 4:05 p.m., the black Escalade remained parked in his assigned spot. The sun was beaming through the windshield, and she had to keep turning on the engine so the A/C could cool her off. *Why did I have to wear black?*

At 5:15 p.m., the black Escalade finally approached the parking lot exit. She immediately scooted lower in her seat and peaked out the driver's side window. There he was, wearing dark sunglasses and bopping his head to the music as he looked both ways before pulling out of the lot. He made a left turn onto the street and quickly sped off.

Adrienne sat up, put the car in drive, and took off behind him while trying to maintain a few car lengths away. The heavy traffic made it easier for her to blend in with the other cars without him noticing. After a couple of miles, the black Escalade turned into the Target parking lot, and Daron pulled into a space on the far-right side. Pulling to the middle of the lot, Adrienne took a space directly in front of the door and sat there until she could devise a plan.

Daron grabbed a cart from outside and pushed it into the store. Adrienne wondered what a man with so much money would be doing in a place such as Target.

After giving him enough time to get inside the store, she quickly walked through the lot and grabbed a cart for herself, then proceeded inside to find him. He was heading down one of the aisles, so she pushed her cart to the next aisle over. As she made her way down the row of kitchen gadgets, she randomly grabbed a few items—a garlic press, can opener, and corkscrew. Then Adrienne turned the corner into the adjacent aisle, where she found Daron examining the merchandise on the shelves as he pushed his cart in her direction. Their eyes met as they approached the middle of the aisle.

"Adrienne, it's you!" said Daron.

Finally, they stood face-to-face again, and he was more handsome than the last time she saw him. Adrienne thought he looked sexy with his dress shirt unbuttoned and his sleeves rolled up. He held his keys in his hand, and his sunglasses sat on top of his head. Smiling, he extended his arms to hug her, and she eagerly embraced him. To her, his tight, muscular frame felt like heaven. She closed her eyes and inhaled his cologne's alluring scent, which immediately triggered that tingly feeling. While appreciating the moment she had long awaited, she almost forgot to let go. He kissed her on the cheek, then took a step back to look at her.

"Wow," he said, looking her up and down. "So, you're a college graduate now. Congratulations!"

"Thank you," she said, blushing.

Her plan was working, and for the next ten minutes, they stood in aisle seven catching up on things going on in their lives. He still owned his insurance agency, as if she didn't already know, and most of the employees she worked with last summer were still there. Then he changed the subject to talk more about her.

"So, are you with anyone?" he asked after looking her up and down several more times.

"Oh, no. I came here alone," she answered.

He tilted his head sideways and then let out a slight chuckle.

"No, I mean, are you seeing anyone?"

Caught off guard with his question, she felt her face turn red and warm. She knew he liked to flirt with her when they worked together; however, she had not expected him to be so forward.

"Oh, uh, I'm not seeing anyone. No," she responded.

She pulled the strap of her purse tighter into her shoulder. She was a little embarrassed by the misunderstanding, but Daron ignored her discomfort and continued.

"Well, I may have some openings at my company soon. If you'd be interested in coming back to work there, I could contact you when something comes up. Why don't you give me your number to call you?"

What? What does that have to do with— Okay, just give him the number.

Adrienne typed her number in his phone and told him she would be excited to work for him again. He placed his phone in his pants pocket and assured her that he would call as soon as a position became available.

Then he added, "Or, if you don't mind, maybe I will call you sooner. You know, so that we can catch up with things?"

Adrienne wanted to scream yes but had to keep her composure. She couldn't let him know how perfect her plan was working.

"Sure. I'm available whenever," she said.

They said their goodbyes, and Adrienne headed towards the checkout. She couldn't wait to get into her car and scream. So far, this was the highlight of what she hoped to be a wonderful summer.

As she drove out the lot, she turned on the radio. There was an old-school hip-hop song playing that immediately reminded her of Daron. She turned up the volume, put on her shades, and bopped her head to the music, thinking of him as she sped through the city streets.

After returning the rental, Adrienne requested a Lyft to take her home. She dreaded the questions her mother would probably have for why she didn't drive her car to work. She just wanted to get to her room and think about Daron. When she walked into the house, her mother was chopping garlic cloves in the kitchen.

"Hey, love. Have you eaten? Dinner's running a little late. Oh, did you stop at Target?" she asked, noticing the bag in Adrienne's hand.

"Yes. I bought you something."

Adrienne placed the Target bag on top of the counter and made a beeline to her room before her mother could interrogate her.

Chapter Eleven

Intimate Conversations

After running into Adrienne at Target, Daron didn't mind going home to an empty house. He had asked for her number and used the excuse that he would call her when a position at his company opened. Seeing how fine she was in the store only reminded him of their conversations last summer, and her gorgeous smile was nothing he could forget. He had no intentions of hiring her again. *Too much drama.* But his temptation to reach out to Adrienne was too much, and the opportunity was too good. Lately, she had been on Daron's mind; he always wanted to explain why he didn't show up for her going away party. *That will give me a good reason to call her tonight.*

After contemplating whether or not to do so, Daron eventually gave in and texted Adrienne. *Can you talk?* It didn't take long before he received the green light, and as he stretched out on the bed with the television on mute, he made the call.

He set the tone to be friendly and cordial. They talked about general topics—what they watched on television, which woman on *Housewives of Atlanta* they favored most, how the frat parties were on campus, and other light-hearted and casual subjects. Before Daron had a chance to bring it up, Adrienne beat him to it and asked about her last day at work.

"I'm so sorry about that day," he said. "Paula reminded me the night before that I had a conference to attend. Apparently, I booked it a while ago and must have forgotten. I would have canceled, except they had me scheduled as a guest panelist, and it would've looked bad if I hadn't shown. I told Paula to tell you that I was very sorry and wished you the best. I honestly thought she'd do the right thing. Then I found the receipt for the gift she got you. I was disappointed because I wanted you to have something nice. That led me to start inquiring about other stuff. Let's just say it was a big mess, but at the time, I didn't think it would be appropriate to try to contact you."

Daron eventually figured out that Paula was trying to keep him away from Adrienne. When he did, he scolded Paula to the point that she almost quit her job. There was a heated argument between them—Daron demanding that Paula mind her business and Paula adamantly defending her actions.

"Look, Daron, I've known you and Linda a long time, and I will not stand by and watch you make a fool of yourself for some young girl who happens to come along."

"Oh, so you admit to setting up that trip to keep me away from the office on Adrienne's last day?"

Paula just stood in front of Daron's desk with her arms folded.

"Next time, mind your damn business and stay out of my way!"

"Fine!"

Paula slammed the door as she exited his office and hurried to her office to pack her things. She grabbed all her personal belongings before storming out the door. She didn't want to quit, but she was not going to stand for Daron disrespecting her when she was only trying to keep him from doing something he might regret later.

Paula took off the next two days without bothering to contact Daron. She was done with D.L. Weathers Insurance as far as she was concerned. She would start looking for another job the following week. In the meantime, she needed the time to herself to sort things out. She thought about Linda. Linda wasn't the easiest to get along with, and she was certainly full of herself at times, but she had always been nice to Paula. For that reason alone, Paula couldn't stand to let Daron betray her as he had done in the past.

Paula was updating her resume when Daron finally called her.

"Look, Paula, things got out of hand, and tempers were flying. I know you were only trying to do what was right, and I want to say I'm sorry."

Paula held the phone in silence. Deep down, she didn't want another job. She was happy working for Daron as she had been all these years. The next day, she returned to work—with a raise. She figured the pay raise was to assure none of this would get back to Linda. In other words, it was hush money.

Adrienne was right. Paula had been up to something all along. *Why couldn't he see through her little scheme sooner? And why did he take Paula back?*

"It's okay. It was a great party anyway," Adrienne replied, then thought to herself, *Maybe he'll replace the mediocre gift I received with something better.*

"Perhaps I can find a way to make it up to you one day," he told her.

Adrienne couldn't stop grinning as she gripped the phone tightly while holding it to her ear. It was a good thing she and Daron weren't talking face-to-face at that moment because he would have seen everything she was thinking on her face.

Something had been on Daron's mind for a long time—something he needed to clear in his head.

"Can I ask you something, Adrienne?"

"Yeah, sure," she responded.

"There were messages written on the street near my house. Do you know anything about that?" he asked, holding his breath.

Adrienne dropped her head. Her first thought was to lie. She didn't want Daron to think she was crazy because she knew it was a crazy thing to do. She had let her heart guide her. No, she wouldn't lie, vowing at that moment to always tell Daron the truth.

"Yeah, I know something about that. I wanted you to know that I was thinking of you."

"One of the messages said you love me," Daron reminded her, wanting to know if it was how she felt.

Adrienne forgot she had written that. Embarrassed, she had to figure a way out of this.

"I love you like a friend. That's what I meant," she said quickly, hoping he would let it go and not torture her with more questions.

Daron smiled; he was thankful for the attention Adrienne showed him. She made him feel important and useful, whereas Linda made him feel like an ornament, a fixture. The attention was welcomed and well reserved.

"Thank you. I appreciated the gesture," Daron replied.

It was Adrienne's turn to smile, glad that he didn't say any more than what he did.

After that night, they fell into a routine. Soon, their text messages and phone calls became more frequent. However, Adrienne noticed certain things about their communication. For instance, Daron rarely told her to call him back whenever he left a voicemail. He would usually say, *I'll call you back when I can,* or *I'll text you tomorrow.* Sometimes, Adrienne would call him back, only to have it go straight to voicemail. There were other times when they would be having a great conversation, laughing and joking, and then suddenly, he would have to hang up abruptly. Adrienne assumed his wife was walking in at that moment, and although it hurt a little, she never spoke about it. She would just patiently wait until he was available again.

As the conversations became more frequent, they began to speak more comfortably. What began as subtle flirting cultivated into intense sexual fantasies, leaving no limits to the imagination. Although she never asked, Adrienne assumed his wife was away promoting books or at some out-of-town conference whenever they spent late nights engaging in hot and steamy sexual exchanges.

The intimate discussions left Adrienne with vivid sexual images of her and Daron on her mind. Adrienne was sometimes so turned on that she became frustrated from not acting on her thoughts. Daron enjoyed their late-night talks, as well, and the following morning, he would send Adrienne a text message letting her know how well he slept thanks to one of their erotic chats.

He often hinted about wishing their fantasies become a reality and frequently ended the conversation with "One day..." or "If only things were different." Adrienne listened while envisioning the different scenarios in her head and hoped someday those fantasies would come true.

The timing could not have been better. Early one afternoon, during one of their talks, Daron mentioned that his wife would be attending a book launch in Atlanta. In response, Adrienne casually said that the two could finally have their chance to make things happen between them. To her surprise, he agreed to take her up on the offer.

"Are you serious?" she asked.

Adrienne wanted him to be, but this seemed too perfect.

"Yes," he replied. "We've been talking about this for a long time. I think we can both agree that we want the same thing."

The fact that he had a wife was no longer a concern for Adrienne. To her, she had already invested much of her time; soon, Linda would have to step aside. Here it was, the opportunity to be with Daron, and she would do whatever it took to ensure it happened.

They spent the rest of the conversation arranging plans for them to meet finally. After hanging up the phone, Adrienne took a deep breath. She was nervous and excited at the same time. There was plenty to do—hair, makeup, lingerie. She would go shopping the next day. In the meantime, she got ready for bed, but with a smile on her face instead of tears in her eyes this night.

Chapter Twelve

Egyptian Cotton

Adrienne gently applied a second coat of the Mocha Passion lipstick and examined it in the mirror. *It never looks the same as when you try it on in the store*, she thought to herself. Disappointed with the newly purchased shade, she grabbed some tissue and wiped the dull color from her lips, then reached into her makeup bag for one of her old favorites. She had already spent too much time at the M.A.C. counter trying to find the perfect lipstick, and now she was running late.

After applying a different shade, Adrienne rummaged through her jewelry box and found the gold heart pendant. It was a gift from her father that she always wore on special occasions, and this night would indeed be special. Once she placed it around her neck and tugged it gently to ensure it was secure, she slipped on a newly purchased gold bracelet to match.

Stepping into the black, off-the-shoulder dress, Adrienne turned around in the mirror to admire her figure. She felt sexy, especially with the new sheer black stockings and garter belt underneath. It was her first time wearing lingerie so seductive.

She never had a need for it, considering she rarely got that far with dating. However, tonight was different, and she wanted to make her best impression.

I've gone overboard for this night, but it's going to be worth it.

After checking herself in the mirror for a few more moments, she grabbed her new clutch and keys and closed her bedroom door as she exited.

"Nice dress! Where are you going?" her mother asked as Adrienne tiptoed down the hall towards the front door.

She was curled up under a blanket in her favorite recliner, the volume on the television low.

"Out."

"This time of night? It's almost midnight."

Adrienne stood about three feet from the front door, trying to think of something to say to put her mother's mind at ease. She knew how inquisitive she could get.

"I'm going to hang out with some friends. I won't be long," Adrienne told her.

Her story was far from the truth. Daron Weathers was the only *friend* she planned to see that night, and if she could help it, it would be a *very* long night.

"Oh? What friends are you going to see this time of night? *Jacki?* Doesn't she have a baby or two to take care of?"

Her mother shifted her body to get a better look at Adrienne. Eyebrows raised, she noticed how tight the black dress wrapped around Adrienne's curves.

"No, Ma, it's not Jacki. Staci and Anthony are having their anniversary party tonight. I already missed the dinner, so I'm going to catch a few dances," Adrienne said.

She sensed her mother's skepticism and feared getting caught in her lies. Without giving her mother a chance to ask any more questions, she walked out the door, quickly shutting it behind her.

Her mother knew something was up. *Doesn't she realize I*

attended Staci and Anthony's wedding? There's something else going on. Why else would she have to lie about where she's going?

Ever since she's been home this summer, things about her seem different. Perhaps her job is stressful. Or maybe she's found a new love.

Her mother shook her head at the thought of Adrienne going out with a new guy and recalled the last one she got involved with.

No, things are better with her now.

She flipped through a few channels until she located the ID Channel. The woman featured in the story reminded her of Adrienne. Starting to worry, her mother quickly changed the channel, hoping Adrienne wasn't falling into the same pattern as she had in the past.

Her mother leaned back in her recliner and sighed. She decided she would wait up for Adrienne.

Just to make sure she gets home safely.

*****

Adrienne jumped into her car and made a quick check of her lipstick in the rearview mirror before driving off. She hated lying to her mother but wouldn't dare admit her real intentions. She was already feeling guilty because she was the one who initiated this rendezvous with Daron. After flirting through text messages and calls over the past few weeks, Adrienne was more than anxious to have time alone with him finally. The sexual tension between the two of them had grown to a level they could no longer refrain. Now it was time to live out those fantasies shared between them.

Adrienne headed down the highway towards the hotel, where she agreed to meet Daron. However, just before getting onto the highway ramp, Daron called her. *Is he chickening out?*

"Hey, Adrienne. Are you on your way?"

Len Richelle

Adrienne's heart started beating fast; she immediately sensed Daron was backing out of their plan.

"I'm almost on the highway. What's up?"

"Change of plans. I know this might sound crazy...well, it is kinda crazy, but can you meet me at my house instead of the hotel?"

Adrienne didn't believe she heard him correctly. *His house? The home where he and Linda lived?*

"Well, sure," Adrienne beamed. "But may I ask why the house?"

"Lots of...I-I don't even know. You know what? Maybe this isn't a good—"

"No! I mean, yes... I'll meet you at your house if that's what you want. I'll be right there. What's your address again?"

*****

Daron could kick himself in the ass for allowing another woman into his home. He'd had some indiscretions before, but he thought he had outgrown dumb shit like this. Linda never found out about him bringing any women to the house. She may have suspected it but never found any proof. Now, after a few too many shots of whiskey, Daron was back to his old tricks.

In his mind, he justified his actions—no other place would be discreet enough. Too many people knew Daron and Linda. *I mean, her face is all over book covers, and mine is plastered on bus stop benches.* Still, he knew it was wrong to bring another woman to his home—the home he shared with his beloved wife.

Yeah, the wife who's never here.

He took one last gulp of his drink before heading to the wine cabinet to pick out a couple of bottles. He planned to bring her only as far as the entertainment room. The oversized couch was big enough for the two of them to get busy. He thought how

90

Linda never stepped foot in that room. She stayed cooped up in her office whenever she was home while Daron waited patiently for attention.

He took one last look around the entertainment room to make sure everything was in place. He envisioned the various sexual positions he would put Adrienne in. The thought of her laid out on the couch started to arouse him, and he hurried up the stairs to get ready before she arrived.

*****

Scarsdale was an affluent suburb north of New York City. Since meeting Daron, Adrienne had become familiar with the area and often drove through there to admire the beautiful mansions on the quiet, tree-lined streets—especially Daron's. Daron lived in the Heathcote section centrally located in the Scarsdale village. Adrienne thought back to when she worked for Daron the previous summer. She had passed by his street, getting a glimpse of the meticulously landscaped yard that accented the million-dollar home and wondering if she could only be lucky enough to step foot inside one day. Tonight, she would fulfill that dream.

Adrienne sped through the secluded streets and turned left onto the private road. There were only two houses on Daron's street, and she turned into the first driveway on the left with the tall, wrought-iron gate. Once inside, she followed the cobblestone driveway leading to the huge Mediterranean-styled home. Finally getting a close-up view, her mouth dropped in amazement at the 6,000-square-foot palace in front of her. As she slowly navigated up the stone pathway, she took in the details of the beautifully landscaped yard. A five-foot-high stucco wall lined with tall, bushy evergreens surrounded the entire property and provided privacy from the outer streets. An array of sculptured shrubbery, colorful rose bushes, and beautiful tropical-looking flowers in large planters decorated the lawn, and small in-ground lamps illuminated the walkway leading to the front door. The closer she got to the house, the more excited she became.

As instructed, she pulled around the side of the house to the three-car garage, turned off the ignition, and waited. In less than a minute, Daron came out from the side of the house and opened her driver's side door.

"Hello, beautiful," he greeted.

He was wearing a black tank top that showed off his chiseled arms and a pair of jeans that fell perfectly over his long, taut legs.

"Hello to you," she responded, smiling flirtatiously as she extended her legs to the ground.

She hadn't realized how short her dress was until she caught a glimpse of the garter attached to her stockings. Daron saw it, too, and tried his best to refrain from showing how eager he was to take another look. He took her hand as she gracefully stepped out of the car.

"You look stunning tonight," Daron complimented.

Adrienne could tell by the lustful look in his eyes that their last phone conversation was still on his mind. They were both looking forward to what was about to transpire.

Still holding his hand, she followed him into the dimly lit house. They walked through the laundry room, which was the size of her kitchen, and she followed him down the hall and into the central part of the home. The house was quite spectacular with its vaulted ceilings, large windows, and terracotta tiled floors. They entered a large room that she assumed was used for entertaining. A huge fireplace flickered with bright orange and yellow flames. Above the fireplace hung an enormous flat-screen television. A six-piece peanut-colored leather sectional with reclining chairs on each end was in the middle of the room. Adrienne took a deep breath as she admired the space surrounding her. She had never been inside a house so magnificent.

"Have a seat. Make yourself comfortable," Daron said.

Adrienne sat on the edge of the soft leather couch. Though she looked forward to the romantic night ahead, she was extremely nervous about the expected encounter.

"Would you like something to drink? Wine?" asked Daron.

Adrienne nodded her head, then slid herself back on the couch to get comfortable. The sound of soft jazz music piped through speakers mounted in the ceiling. The acoustics were so clear that it sounded like the band was playing right in the room.

Daron walked over to the bar and poured two glasses of wine. The flames from the fireplace illuminated the room, and it was bright enough for her to make out his sculptured abs protruding through his body-hugging tank top. As he faced the bar, she caught a glimpse of his rear assets, as well, and could only imagine what was inside those perfectly fitting jeans. She wanted to skip over the small talk because their earlier phone call was so sexually intense that she thought she would explode before making it through the door.

They drank a couple of glasses of wine while listening to the music. By the second glass, Adrienne was relaxed and ready. Daron took her wine glass and placed it on the table in front of them. They stared into each other's eyes as he gently held her hands. In a matter of seconds, they were passionately kissing and caressing each other as Daron carefully lay her on the couch.

"I've been waiting for this for so long," he whispered.

His breathing became heavier as he glided his hands up and down her body. Adrienne tried to be patient as he slowly undressed her, but the anticipation of having this man inside her was too much. She no longer felt like the shy young girl anymore, and after unhooking the latch on her dress, she turned her back towards him so he could zip it down. They alternated taking off one piece of each other's clothing, tossing each piece aimlessly on the floor. In no time, they were completely naked.

Standing up from the couch, he took her hand and pulled her up. As he led her down the hallway, she shivered as the coldness of the floor tingled her feet and sent chills through her body. Squeezing his hand tightly, Adrienne followed him up the curved staircase to the second floor.

At the top of the stairs was a pedestal holding a tall, bronze statue of a nude man and woman entwined with one another. The woman had long, flowing hair and a slim yet curvaceous body, while the man was tall with a muscular physique. Assuming it was a sculpture of Daron and his wife, Adrienne admired the intricate details of the male figure's body. There were double doors next to the statue that led to a huge master bedroom. Inside the room was another fireplace that emitted enough light to reveal the king-sized bed and a variety of fluffed pillows.

Still holding her hand, he began walking into the room, but Adrienne gently pulled him back with hesitation. As much as she wanted him, the thought of having sex in the bed he shared with his wife was taking it too far. It was bad enough their tryst would happen in their marital home.

For a moment, he looked at her in silence as if he had read her mind. He nodded, then letting go of her hand, he walked into the bedroom alone. She stood there naked in the hallway, still shivering from the cold floor yet heated with passion. She watched as he pulled back the thick, white duvet that covered the bed. There was just enough light from the fireplace to see him lie on his back in the center of the bed. His penis was fully erect as he looked in her direction, waiting.

Leaving behind any dignity and self-respect she had, Adrienne slowly walked into the room and climbed onto the king-sized bed. She nestled in between the Egyptian cotton sheets and relished in the soft, warm material as it touched her skin. They looked into each other's eyes as he pulled the top sheet over their bodies and pulled her closer to his nude frame.

As they took their time getting to know each other's

physique, Adrienne took a quick glimpse around the room. It was about half the size of the entire floor of her mother's house and contained two walk-in closets, a bathroom, and a balcony with a view that overlooked the front yard.

Wow was all she could think of to describe what she was feeling.

He continued to caress her skin as she took in the details of the room's contemporary furnishings. He gently kissed her neck and massaged her breasts; she placed her arms around his solid frame and gently glided her fingertips up and down the center of his back.

As he pleasured her with his hands, she looked around the room for any indications of what his wife was like. There was a framed picture of the couple on top of the armoire, but it was too dark to see her face. On the long dresser was a vanity tray with several fancy perfumes, and only inches away on the nightstand was a tiny porcelain statuette of a woman holding a book. Things that should have stopped her from going any further only excited her more, and she pulled him on top of her and let him in.

*****

4:05 A.M.

She squinted, trying to focus as she read the time on the alarm clock on the nightstand next to her. Adrienne woke up savoring the previous night's passion. She lay on her back, looking up at the darkness as she imagined the possibilities for the future.

This is us every night—making love between the 1,500-thread count sheets into the wee hours of the morning. We oversleep and arrive late for work, but that's okay because we own the company. As we pass each other in the office hallway at work, we gently touch each other's fingertips and exchange dreamy smiles while silently reminiscing about the previous night's passion.

She lay there for a few minutes contemplating when to get up and what time to leave. She watched Daron's chest move up and down with deep, quiet breaths. He was just as attractive sleeping as he was awake. She wanted to wake him up so they could have another round before the sun came up but also wanted to be back home before her mother woke up. By now, her mother would've figured out she lied about attending an anniversary party. She would be up in a couple of hours, so it was better to sneak into the house now to delay the confrontation.

After about fifteen minutes, Adrienne quietly snuck down the stairs to the entertainment room and found her clothes still on the floor. Once dressed, she tiptoed down the hall and out through the side door. It would have been nice to have a kiss goodbye or even be escorted to her car, but considering the situation she was in, it was better to leave discreetly.

Just as she hoped, her mother and Kara were still asleep by the time she got home. So, she crept into her bed and slept through the morning.

By 11:30 a.m., she was awakened by the sound of her mother banging pots and pans in the kitchen. She figured her mother had realized Adrienne hadn't gone to an anniversary party and was upset about her lying about where she was going.

Adrienne rolled over and sat up against her two pillows, which weren't half as fluffy as Daron's. Reflecting on the previous night's encounter, she smiled while stretching out her arms and legs. Then she stood to go to the bathroom, hoping to avoid her mother in the process.

After showering, Adrienne slipped back into her bedroom and lay across the bed. Grabbing her cell phone, she checked to see if she had any missed messages and discovered a couple of texts from Jacki, and most importantly, a message from

Daron:

Hey, love. Missed you this morning. Don't leave me like that again. Woke up ready for you.

Smiling from ear to ear, Adrienne immediately responded back, *Sorry, babe. Had to run. Will make it up to you ANYTIME. XOXO.*

As she pressed the send button, she heard footsteps stop in front of her door. It was her mother coming to interrupt her happy thoughts.

"How was the anniversary party?" she asked, standing in the doorway with her hand on her hip.

The glare in her mother's eyes said everything. Adrienne slyly looked up, then returned to scrolling through her phone.

"I need you to take your sister to the church. She has choir practice today."

Adrienne didn't bother to look up. She wanted to avoid the "conversation" by any means.

"Okay," she answered politely.

Suddenly, Adrienne's phone chimed. She opened the text message from Daron, who responded with three red hearts. She squealed with delight, then slid back under the covers to dream about the night before. *Hmm, Egyptian cotton.*

Chapter Thirteen
Filled with Frustration

Daron woke up to an empty bed yet again. *Even Adrienne leaves me high and dry.* In a way, Daron thought it was good that she was already gone. He didn't need that awkward good morning ritual that comes with sleeping with someone for the first time—especially in the bed he shared with his wife.

He sat up and tried to process the night before. He cheated on his wife. *Again.* It had been a while since the last affair; they eventually worked through it, and Linda forgave him. *But why now?* Turning all the blame towards his wife, he started mentally listing all the things that hadn't been going well between him and Linda. *It's those goddamn books. She's always out of town.*

He'd been feeling neglected and unappreciated for quite a while now. With all his built-up sexual tension and steamy conversations with Adrienne, he was about to burst if he didn't act on it. *Damn, dude.*

Daron shook off any feelings of regret and decided to send Adrienne a text. He could still smell her scent, and it quickly aroused him. *I better remember to change these sheets.*

*****

When Daron arrived home from work Monday evening, Linda's car was in the garage. He was happy to have his wife home and hoped they could sit down and have a long talk. As he walked into the house, an aroma of juicy filet mignon floated through the air. Linda was in the kitchen making all his favorite foods.

"Babe, you're just in time," Linda said.

She wiped her hands on a dishtowel and wrapped her arms around his neck. He hugged her waist, then slid his hands down to grab her butt cheeks that fit so perfectly in his hands. He had missed her the past few days, despite the adulterous company he kept.

"Mmm," Daron moaned, enjoying the moment. "I'm so happy to see you," he said while hugging her, even as a flashback of Adrienne haunted him.

He refused to let the guilt overcome him, though. *No, not tonight.* He lifted Linda's chin to kiss her soft lips.

"Dinner will be ready in a couple of minutes. Put your things down, and I'll fix your plate."

Daron placed his jacket and messenger bag at the bottom of the steps, then went into the downstairs bathroom to wash up. Glimpsing in the mirror, he smiled—looking forward to spending the evening with his wife.

They sat across from each other in the kitchen nook. Linda seldom liked eating in the dining room unless they had company. It was frustrating to Daron because he had spent several thousands of dollars on the dining room set and the perfect place settings Linda insisted they buy.

Daron sliced his filet mignon while Linda talked about her trip. He enjoyed having these evenings with his wife, and it hurt him that they had become so seldom. Linda seemed to be in a great mood. She was talkative, lively, and even laughed a few times during the conversation. Daron felt it was the perfect time to bring up something he'd had on his mind lately.

"Baby, do you think you could put off some of your book promotions for a while? I've really been missing you."

He thought about how humble he sounded, practically begging his wife for attention.

Linda slowly placed her knife and fork on the sides of her plate and wiped the corners of her mouth with the linen napkin. She avoided looking directly at Daron as she took her time responding—as if to select the right words. Then she cleared her throat, reached her hand across the table, and placed it on top of Daron's.

"Do you remember when you first opened up your office?"

"Yes," he replied.

"Do you know how much I sacrificed to support you? I mean, sure, I taught at the university, but that wasn't exactly my dream job. I only did that so we could have a steady income and benefits. Now it's my turn to shine."

Putting a period on the conversation, Linda took a sip of her wine and continued eating.

Daron was left feeling stunned and disappointed. He hoped to hear that his wife cared enough to want to invest in spending more time together, but she made it known that she had no intentions of slowing down. Suddenly, Daron lost his appetite. Without another word, he pushed away his plate and went upstairs.

After a long, hot shower, Daron went into the entertainment room and lay across the sectional to watch TV. He couldn't stop feeling frustrated about his wife and her not trying to understand how he felt.

This is supposed to be a marriage.

While he stared at the television screen, unaware of what show was playing, his cell phone chimed, indicating he had a text message. It was from Adrienne.

Chapter Fourteen

Secret Lovers

Adrienne wanted more than anything to tell someone about her new romance—whether Staci, Jacki, or even her sister, Kara. She didn't know how long she could keep it to herself. Yet, she knew everyone would judge her. They'd just think things would end badly like her last relationship, and Staci would probably go as far as to warn Adrienne's mother. *They will probably try to have an intervention or something.*

No, she'd wait. For now, she would keep them at bay and not disclose much about Daron. *At least not until the divorce is in the works.* There was just too much at stake to have her family and friends ruin it for her.

"What's up? You seem preoccupied with something," said Jacki.

They had been on the phone for about forty-five minutes, and Jacki had done most of the talking. Adrienne barely said one word as she could not stop thinking about her newfound love. She hadn't heard from Daron since receiving the text from him the day after the night they spent together and worried if she had done something to push him away. She knew he was a busy man, and most of all, he had a wife. However, she still felt she was owed a conversation or two now and then.

"Huh? Oh, I guess I'm a little tired, that's all."

"Did you even hear what I said? I'm asking your opinion. Do you think it's a good idea or what?"

Adrienne was a bit confused. She didn't know what she was responding to but didn't want Jacki to know she had ignored her during their conversation.

"Roderick's a nice guy. I say give him another chance."

For a moment, all Adrienne could hear on the other end of the phone was the television and Jacki's little boys playing in the background.

"Hello?" said Adrienne.

"I guess I'll talk to you later," Jacki replied, the angry tone in her voice suddenly getting Adrienne's attention. "And by the way, I was talking about Kevin and asking what I should take when I meet his parents for dinner. I haven't dated Roderick in a month."

Adrienne heard silence and realized Jacki had disconnected the call.

She felt horrible. Adrienne hadn't been paying attention to her family or friends lately. Now Jacki was pissed at her, and knowing Jacki, she would stay pissed for a while.

Oh well. Adrienne sighed and placed her phone on her nightstand. For now, all she was concerned about was waiting for Daron to call.

*****

"I've missed you," said Adrienne.

She tried to refrain from sounding too excited when Daron finally called. The following weekend, he responded to her last text message, and as soon as she heard his voice, she did everything she could to contain herself.

"Sorry, Adrienne. I've been so busy," he told her, then added, "I've been thinking about you, though."

Adrienne heard just what she needed. *He wants me.* Her heart raced as she imagined herself back in his arms.

"Well, when can we get together again?"

Adrienne's questions caught Daron off guard. As much lust as he felt for Adrienne, he wasn't ready to take another chance on a second encounter.

"I–I don't know if we should right now. Adrienne, maybe you don't understand. I like you a lot, but I have a wife. It's just not that easy."

Adrienne felt the lump in her throat. His words hurt, but at the same time, it made her want him even more.

"That's okay. Whenever you have time."

She didn't like the feeling of rejection, but she wasn't giving up on him. He was perfect for her.

As he hung up the phone, Daron wondered, *What have I gotten myself into?* Adrienne was fun, lively, and sexy as hell––a reminder of what his wife used to be. *The Linda I used to have fun with.* Despite his miserable marriage, he knew what he was doing with Adrienne would lead to nothing but trouble. However, something about her made him feel alive again.

Two weeks later, Daron made his move.

"Are you busy?"

Adrienne was pulling out of the parking lot of her job. She was on her lunch break when Daron called her cell phone.

"No. Just on my way to get lunch. What's up?" she asked, grinning from ear to ear.

"Well, I thought we could spend a little time together. You know, like last time."

The thought of that night flashed in her mind and gave her that familiar tingling feeling. The thought of the two of them lying between those Egyptian cotton sheets thrilled her.

"Sure," she replied. "Are you home now?"

As Adrienne spoke, she drove past the deli she planned to

order from and headed towards the thruway ramp, the quickest way to Daron's house.

"Oh, no, no, no. We can't go there. My wife is in town. Besides, I'm headed to the mall across town. I thought maybe you could meet me there."

"At the mall?" she asked. "What are we gonna do there?"

Daron hesitated. His idea was absurd yet exciting. Besides, it was the quickest thing he could think of to get what he needed to get done.

"How about meeting me in the lot near the entrance of Home Goods? We'll figure something out from there."

Adrienne was confused and disappointed. She had been looking forward to seeing Daron over the past two weeks, but the *mall*?

"I'll be there in ten minutes," she said.

Adrienne got off at the next exit and sped through the streets until she arrived at the mall. She spotted the black Escalade idling in one of the parking spaces near the Home Goods store, but when she pulled into the lot, the Escalade backed out of the space. Daron extended his hand out of the driver's window and motioned for her to follow. They drove up the parking garage ramp to a more secluded area, and he pulled into a spot far away from the mall entrance. Following his lead, Adrienne pulled up next to him. Daron jumped out of the driver's side, opened his back door, and hopped in.

Adrienne waited a few seconds to see what would happen next but then realized *this* was Daron's plan – to do it in the parking lot. She'd rather the two of them be lying in the king-sized bed; however, she knew she had to win Daron over any way she could. *Besides, it's obvious he's into me.*

After some hesitation, she quickly jumped into the back of the truck, where Daron was waiting with his pants pulled below his knees. His erection and lustful facial expression greeted her.

About forty-five minutes later, Adrienne left the garage and hurried back to work. She no longer needed lunch; she was filled with happiness. Daron seemed so grateful to make love to her—like there was no one else in the world he wanted. *I knew he'd find me irresistible.*

One week later, they met up again. This time, Adrienne was on her way to the store before it closed. Daron called her as she was leaving her house.

"I need to see you *right now*," he told her.

Adrienne could hear the desperation in his voice and eagerly agreed to meet him.

"I'm heading to the Westchester. Do you want me to come over?"

"No," said Daron, "but I'll think of somewhere. I'm in the mood for something *crazy*."

Adrienne interpreted that as him wanting another public tryst. It tickled her that this older, established man had so much lust for her. She didn't mind, though. She knew it would be over between him and Linda soon. *It's just a matter of time.*

"Well, text me with a location. I have a pair of Michael Kors shoes that need to be return—"

Before she had the chance to finish, Daron interrupted.

"I'll meet you there."

"You'll meet me where? At the Michael Kors store?" she asked.

"No, outside. In the lot," he replied,

"I'll call you when I get there."

Adrienne disconnected the call. *Are we doing it at the Westchester?* It wasn't exactly her idea of a romantic evening, but being with him was all that mattered. She freshened up, and ignoring her mother's *where-are-you-going* routine, she headed out the door. As soon as she pulled into the lot, Daron called her cell phone.

"Hey, where are you?" she asked.

"Meet me at P6, near Neiman Marcus," he replied.

Adrienne drove up several ramps to the P6 section of the

garage, where she spotted Daron's Escalade parked a few feet away from the mall entrance. Once again, he pulled out while motioning for her to follow him up several more ramps. Only a few cars were parked on this level, and they pulled into the two spaces against a corner wall. Daron got out of his truck and hopped into the backseat, and like last time, Adrienne followed. This time, she knew what to expect.

"Hey there," she said brightly.

As soon as she got in, he leaned over and planted a moist kiss on her lips. He slowly moved his tongue into her mouth while his hands caressed her body.

She had been looking forward to being with Daron again, and now, the thought of making love in the parking lot of one of the most exclusive malls felt exhilarating. Ready to give all of herself to him, she eagerly slid off her jeans and panties; he had already pulled his pants down below his knees.

Daron said nothing as he lifted her by her waist and positioned her over his midsection. He looked directly into her eyes while gently inserting himself inside her. The eye contact between them reminded Adrienne of the first day she met Daron; he had the most beautiful amber eyes then, and they were even more beautiful now.

As she felt his hardness inside her, she slowly moved her body up and down, then gradually increased the pace. Sliding off Adrienne's shirt and bra, Daron began caressing her breasts, taking turns kissing and sucking each one with the utmost passion. Adrienne leaned in closer to him, teasing him with her tongue and running her fingers through his freshly-cut waves. She could feel his warm breath tingling down her neck as he whispered passionately in her ear.

"You feel so good, baby. Yes, baby, that's it."

He needed her, and she could hear it in his voice as he called out her name. She sensed Daron hadn't felt this good in a long time, and seeing him squirm in ecstasy turned her on. She began moving her hips even faster as she clawed her acrylic nails deep into his shoulders. With every stroke, Daron pulled her down harder and harder, causing Adrienne to sink her teeth into the side of his neck as she enjoyed the painful yet pleasurable experience. Daron moaned even louder, and they continued thrusting vigorously in harmony. Suddenly, Adrienne began to lose control—no longer caring about where she was, who was watching, or how she looked. She wanted nothing more than to enjoy this man inside her. She threw her head back, lifted her arms over her head to grab the headrest behind her, and began to thrust as hard as she could. Her soft, refrained moans soon became loud, uninhibited screams as the waves of pleasure came over her. In no time, she collapsed while still on top of Daron, weak and shaking, completely spent.

"Damn, baby. What's gotten into you?" asked Daron.

She opened her eyes to see his face drenched with sweat, half grinning, and looking impressed with his young lover. They spent the next few minutes recuperating until Adrienne realized she still had to return the shoes. She looked at her watch and saw it was ten minutes to nine.

"I have to go. The store is about to close," she said.

She hopped off Daron's lap, grabbed her panties and jeans, and quickly slid them on. Daron, who was still trying to catch his breath, kissed her softly on the lips before she returned to her car to retrieve the shopping bag from the trunk. She ran down the ramp until she got to the Neiman Marcus entrance, then rushed through the store and into the mall to find the Michael Kors store. She made it there one minute before closing.

That evening was the second of many spur-of-the-moment meetups in various parking garages around Westchester County. They began seeing each other several times a week, often during lunchtime or late in the evening before Daron returned home for the night. It was not the dream house and the king-sized bed Adrienne imagined she'd go back to, but she quietly accepted the routine and always waited for Daron's call.

After their lovemaking, they would sometimes spend a few moments cuddling and talking. At first, the conversations were lighthearted. They talked about their days at work and any plans for the weekend, just like when she worked for him the previous summer. Eventually, Daron began to open up to Adrienne regarding issues in his marriage. At first, it bothered Adrienne because she didn't like Daron using their quality time to discuss his problems with Linda. But she listened in silence as he vented about their marital frustrations. Gradually, Adrienne saw Daron's ranting about his wife as an opportunity for herself. It was her way in. Eager to win him over, she listened to every detail and egged Daron on when he spoke negatively about Linda. The more Adrienne listened, the more her own opinions formed about how terrible his wife was. Daron complained about Linda traveling too much, and although his insurance company was financially successful and a well-established business in the community, Linda always seemed to push her way into the spotlight. There were small things Linda did that he disliked, and he pointed them out to Adrienne. Then he would commend her for not doing the same things Linda did. Adrienne was hopeful that Daron would finally see he was much better off with her than with his wife. It was just a matter of time.

"What did she do this time?" she asked whenever he appeared upset or frustrated.

Adrienne would shake her head in disgust and make Daron believe Linda's actions were despicable.

"I can't believe she would do something like that. I couldn't imagine doing something like that to you."

It seemed Daron was falling right into Adrienne's trap, and she was ready to catch him.

From Adrienne's perspective, she and Daron had a future together. There was never a discussion about their relationship status, except when Daron had to remind Adrienne that he was married. It usually occurred when Adrienne would demand more time with him or when she complained about meeting in the backseat of his truck. However, Adrienne patiently waited for her day to come. *It's only a matter of time.* For now, just as Daron insisted, things would be discreet between them. *If Linda were to find out about us now, she would try to take all his money.* So, Adrienne respected Daron's request for secrecy.

Daron and Adrienne continued their routine for the next few months. He'd text her to meet him, giving twenty minutes' notice, and Adrienne found herself racing to the designated parking garage to help him forget about his troubles. However, as the fall season brought cooler weather, Adrienne grew tired of the last-minute trysts in his truck. She looked forward to something more romantic, like spending time together in front of the warm fireplace in his Heathcote home.

"When are we going to go back to your house?" she asked one evening.

They were sitting in the backseat of Daron's truck, and Adrienne was straddling his lap while seducing him with a striptease. Daron eagerly licked his lips as he watched her hypnotizing movements. He immediately jolted from his sexual spell and sunk down in the seat. Inviting Adrienne to his house was only meant to happen one time; he never planned for it to happen again. Taking her to a hotel was still out of the question. He was too paranoid about being recognized or, even worse, having security cameras recording their every move. As far as he was concerned, they were safe in the back of his truck in the middle of a parking garage.

"You know we have to be careful," he said, then slid down his boxers to continue what they started.

Adrienne pushed away from him and pulled the straps of her bra back onto her shoulders. She clutched her blouse close to her chest as she moved to the opposite corner. Plopping down into the seat, Adrienne sulked and stared out at the nearly empty garage. The two sat in silence until Daron realized his night was not going to go as expected. It was selfish of him, but at this point, he couldn't face going home unsatisfied. *Think of something quick before the mood dies entirely.* He took a deep sigh, then gently placed his hand on her thigh before reluctantly responding.

"Wait until she leaves for Key Largo. She'll be flying down next Sunday for the winter, and we'll have the house to ourselves then," Daron told her, although he knew he might regret it later.

Letting Adrienne have access to his private life meant nothing but danger. He didn't want her to get comfortable coming to his house. It was just way too risky, let alone disrespectful. Yet, on a sexual level, he felt he would do almost anything to please her just as she pleased him.

*****

For Adrienne, Sunday could not come fast enough. She spent the whole week prepping for the occasion—getting her hair and nails done, a pedicure, and picking out the perfect lingerie for the evening. She could barely make it through the week without thinking about the time they would spend together. Finally, that Sunday evening, she got the text she had been waiting to receive. He had dropped off his wife at the airport that morning and instructed Adrienne to meet him. This time, it wasn't in a parking garage.

Pull into the driveway. I'll meet you at the side door.

To avoid standing in the cold, she waited until he appeared at the door. Adrienne then grabbed her overnight bag from the passenger's seat, and without saying a word, she walked behind him through the laundry room, bypassing the entertainment room. She followed Daron as he headed up the stairs to the master bedroom illuminated by the flickering orange flames of the fireplace. This time, she didn't hesitate to enter. She knew what she wanted, and it didn't matter what room they were in as long as she got it.

*****

After Daron fell fast asleep, Adrienne slowly pulled back the sheets, slipped on her lingerie, and quietly tiptoed out into the hall. She never got the chance to see the entire house, so now was the perfect time to explore.

The dim lighting in the hallway allowed her to find her way around, and she roamed curiously to the other end of the second floor. She flicked on a light and entered another bedroom with a large four-poster bed and a huge walk-in closet. Inside the closet were fancy coats and shelves full of winter boots and other winter accessories. She circled the rest of the room, gently running her fingertips along the crystal and porcelain figurines displayed on the dresser and shelves. A Jack and Jill bathroom led into another bedroom on the left side of the room.

After exiting that room, she walked into another room across the hall. *Another bedroom.* Next to that room was another bathroom, followed by another bedroom. All the rooms looked like they had never been slept in and were perfectly decorated as if they were featured in the latest issue of *Home and Garden.* Adrienne couldn't imagine why two people needed so many bedrooms, let alone a house so huge. Still, she couldn't help but to wish it all belonged to her.

She crept downstairs and wandered through the rooms of the first floor. Those rooms were also immaculate, and from the small amount of light, she could see that all the furniture looked new and expensive. Making her way into the extra-large kitchen, Adrienne roamed around, gliding her fingers across the white quartz countertops and stainless-steel appliances. The middle island was larger than her kitchen table, and she sat on one of the barstools imagining the meals she would someday cook for Daron. After peeking inside the refrigerator, she opened a few cabinet doors, noting several sets of flatware and expensive-looking drinking glasses. On one of the walls in the kitchen was a small bulletin board with several reminders on sticky notes: *Pick up dry cleaning. Leave money for landscaper. Turn off sprinklers.* All the notes appeared to be in a woman's handwriting.

Underneath the bulletin board was a small cabinet drawer. She slowly pulled it out and carefully rummaged through the items inside. There were small items such as batteries, pens, and a couple of keyrings. Adrienne picked up one set of keys and looked at the tag. Unable to make out the writing on the tag, she opened the refrigerator door and held it in the light. *HOUSE.*

She placed the keyring back in the drawer and slowly closed it before moving on to the next room adjacent to the kitchen. Adrienne assumed it was Linda's office because it had a large desk with two computers and an array of books on a shelf. The room had a feminine touch with brightly-colored pillows that accented a white leather chaise lounge, floral prints on the walls, and a faint smell of perfume lingered in the air.

Adrienne walked to the desk and sat in the white leather and chrome swivel chair. She visualized Linda sitting in front of her laptop as she created her novels. Adrienne swung the chair around to face the large bay window behind her. There was a view of the backyard, and she could see the shimmering waves from the swimming pool as the full moon reflected off the water. She stood up to take a closer look and dreamed of one day basking in the sun after taking a swim in the Roman-shaped pool. It looked so peaceful and tranquil. *I bet it's temperature controlled.*

Looking around the room, she saw many photos, plaques, and awards adorning the walls. She could barely read the words as she squinted in the dark but learned that Linda was Writer of the Year, *best in something*, and had *outstanding achievement* in something else. Some of the awards and plaques had *Linda Weathers, Ph.D.* engraved on them. Others bore the name Lauren Lash, her pen name. Many photos were of Linda posing with men and women who appeared to be very important people in suits, and Daron was by her side in every shot. Adrienne frowned as she stared at the photos.

Suddenly, she noticed the sun beginning to rise. Having been downstairs roaming around for a while, she tried to hurry and get back to bed before Daron noticed she was gone. However, the house was so big that she got lost and couldn't find the stairs. She almost panicked after hearing movement coming from the floor above her. After circling the first floor, she found the staircase near the front entrance. Before running up the stairs, she stopped to look at a large, framed photo hanging on the wall near the door. There was just enough light in the hallway for her to get a closer look at Linda—a beautiful, fair-skinned woman who smiled as if she were the happiest woman in the world. Standing behind her was Daron, his arms tightly wrapped around her waist. Adrienne noticed the large diamond ring and wedding band on Linda's finger. She wondered how much Daron paid for such an expensive-looking ring, then wondered if she would ever be worth that much to him. She hoped one day she would be as she tiptoed back up the stairs.

Chapter Fifteen

The Ultimate Gift – Reality Check

With Christmas just around the corner, Adrienne looked forward to spending it with Daron. Wanting to impress him with the perfect gift, she woke up one Saturday morning to get an early start on shopping for it. After spending hours running from store to store, she was happy to take a break when she received a phone call from Staci asking to meet with her and Jacki for lunch. She agreed, and the three of them met at the Cheesecake Factory nearby.

"So, ladies, I hope you're getting your dresses ready for the party. It's going to be even bigger than last year," said Staci as they waited for their meals.

Adrienne had completely forgotten about Staci's New Year's Eve party. She was so focused on Daron that she hadn't even thought about shopping for something to wear. Staci's parties were phenomenal, and the New Year's Eve party was always the biggest bash in town. The couple knew many people—especially other doctors that her husband, Anthony, worked with—as well as lawyers and other professionals from the local area. Their guests would be seen pulling up in expensive cars and dressed in tuxedos, long gowns, and fur coats. Jacki and Adrienne didn't quite fit in with the upscale crowd, but Staci wouldn't have it any other way than to have her two best friends there with her to enjoy the annual event. Adrienne loved attending her parties, and for her and Jacki, the New Year's Eve event was like prom night all over again. They would start shopping for dresses in October because it usually took a couple of months to find the right one that looked expensive but fit within their budgets. Then they would shop around for the shoes and try different hairstyles and accessories to achieve the perfect look. They enjoyed mingling with Staci's guests while enjoying the live jazz band and delicious platters of mini quiches, smoked salmon rillettes, caviar, and other hors d'oeuvres passed around. Then they would indulge in a buffet of dishes such as Lobster Ravioli, Argentinian Skirt Steak, and Chicken Portabella for the main course.

"I bought my dress," Jackie happily replied. "Todd helped me pick it out. It's so beautiful!"

Staci and Jacki then turned to Adrienne, waiting for the update on her dress selection.

"Oh, Daron bought a beautiful dress for me while we were Christmas shopping," she said casually.

"So, you're bringing Daron? Are we finally going to get to meet him?" Staci asked, shifting in her chair and leaning in closer.

Adrienne hesitated to respond. She had just set herself up to have to tell another pack of lies.

"Of course, he'll be there with me. He's pretty excited about it himself," she said.

Adrienne gulped down the rest of her iced tea, wishing she had ordered alcohol instead. She always tried to impress her friends— mainly because they were a few years older than her and seemed to have more accomplishments and experiences. And since the "incident", she felt she had something to prove. When she first mentioned she was dating a man named Daron, they were skeptical at first, but she talked him up to a point where they both became fond of her mystery man and couldn't wait to meet him. Since then, Adrienne had been throwing his name around yet leaving out the most important detail; he was married.

"I still can't believe I haven't met him yet, and I live right down the street from you," Jacki added.

"I know, Jacki," Adrienne replied dryly. "Don't worry. Everyone will get to meet him on New Year's Eve."

Adrienne knew Daron attending was out of the question. He would never show up at a public event with her. She decided to come up with a story so that Daron somehow couldn't attend at the last minute—just like for her college graduation.

She hoped this would be the end of the conversation about Daron for the rest of the day. Trying to hide the truth was too much work.

By the end of lunch, she came up with the perfect idea for Daron's gift. She returned to the mall and spent about forty-five minutes at the Macy's jewelry counter before finding one she loved. Of course, she knew she couldn't afford the Movado watch, but she wanted so badly to impress Daron. She decided she would scale back on gifts for her mother and Kara. *After all, he's worth it.*

*****

Daron and Adrienne spent several nights together in his home while his wife vacationed hundreds of miles away in Florida. Adrienne noticed how Daron rarely mentioned Linda's name anymore, and she anticipated hearing him say the words "I love you" at any moment.

Then we'll make plans for him to leave his wife.

Adrienne was already playing it out in her mind: *Linda calls Daron to discuss her plans to return to New York, but before she begins, Daron interrupts her with the news. He tells Linda that he is in love with someone else and wants a divorce. Linda demands to know who the homewrecker is, but Daron comes to my defense and confesses that he has been in love with me for a very long time. He tells Linda that I am more of a woman than she ever was and have always been there for him. After several minutes of screaming and yelling, threatening to take Daron for every penny he has, Linda comes to her senses. She realizes she has not been a good wife and understands why Daron would fall in love with someone like me. She grants him the divorce and settles for the house in the Keys and a few items from the home in New York. Daron ships the rest of Linda's belongings to her in Florida so she will not need to return.*

It excited her as she imagined the play-by-play action. She pictured herself moving into the house. Kara would miss her, and her mother would probably be worried since she always found reasons to be concerned about Adrienne these days. Jacki and Staci would be jealous. *I can't wait to see the look on Staci and Jacki's faces at our first holiday party.*

The Saturday before Christmas, Adrienne and Daron made their usual plans to spend the evening together. Like every weekend, Adrienne drove to his house and met him at the side door. She had become very comfortable making her way around the house by now and walked straight upstairs to the bedroom, toting her overnight bag. This time, she had the neatly wrapped Christmas gift hidden in the inside pocket. She decided to wait until the next day to give it to him and make him promise not to open it until they were together on Christmas morning.

They spent the evening engaging in lustful bliss. When she awoke early Sunday morning, the sweet aroma of homemade waffles wafted in the air. Adrienne smiled as she sat up in the bed, stomach rumbling with hunger yet still yearning for Daron's touch. As she gazed around the room, she noticed the door to Daron's walk-in closet was open. On the closet floor lay a large suitcase with clothing sticking out from the sides. It appeared as if he had tossed the luggage in the closet. Curious,

Adrienne walked into the closet to peek inside. T-shirts, shorts, a couple of pairs of swimming trunks, and other warm-weather clothing filled the overstuffed luggage. As she rummaged through the items, she noticed the side pocket where two small, gift-wrapped boxes were carefully placed. One box was a light blue box with "Tiffany & Co." imprinted on the top. She held the box up to her ear and shook it while trying to guess its contents. Tempted to open the gift, she gently tugged on the white ribbon but then quickly placed it back into the side pocket. She didn't want to spoil her surprise.

Is it finally happening?

She hurried to the bed and slid back under the covers, wondering when he would pop the question. She started to giggle as she imagined various scenarios.

I can't wait to see Mom's face when I show her the ring. Now Jacki and Staci will have the chance to meet him. They'll be so jealous! All of my dreams are finally coming true!

A few minutes later, Daron walked into the room carrying a large serving tray of food. They sat up in the bed and indulged in the Belgian waffles, turkey bacon, eggs, and freshly squeezed orange juice he prepared for them. Adrienne tried to hide the slight grin on her face, but Daron noticed.

"Why such a big grin on your face?" he asked.

"Oh, the food. It's so good."

He thanked her for the compliment, kissed her lightly on the cheek, and continued to eat. Occasionally, he would look at her but remained silent. He knew he had to tell her but dreaded doing so because he knew it would break her heart. *I should have set things straight long before now.*

They finished breakfast and continued watching a movie on Netflix as she lay on his chest. Adrienne noticed he kept getting notifications on his cell phone; she could only assume Linda was checking up on him. He did not respond, and she was glad to see all his focus was on her.

When the movie ended, Daron got up to take a shower.

Adrienne usually left after breakfast, but she was expecting to exchange gifts today. She couldn't wait for her surprise. When he got out of the shower, he put on his boxers and a t-shirt, then slipped on a pair of jeans and socks.

"Aren't you going to get dressed?"

"Oh," she said. "Already?"

Adrienne flipped back the covers. Daron usually waited for her to leave before getting dressed. *Why is he in a rush?*

"Well, I have a plane to catch."

She let the words sink in for a moment. *It's a few days before Christmas. Where could he possibly be going now?*

"What do you mean? Where are you going?"

She had asked the question, but she didn't want to hear the answer because she already knew. It was her biggest fear.

"I'm going to join my wife for Christmas in the Keys."

Daron's voice was cold. He knew he would have to bring it up at some point. Now he just wanted to get it over with.

Adrienne sat silently as her heart raced. Her hands, now hot and sweaty, trembled as she pulled the loose strands of hair back behind her ears, hoping perhaps she hadn't heard clearly. He pulled out the stuffed suitcase from the closet floor and placed it on top of the bed along with another smaller carry-on.

Adrienne slowly dressed as she stared at the inside pocket where the two small gifts were tucked away.

Did the entire time we spent together mean anything to him?

There was always something to remind her that he was still a married man who loved his wife—no matter how many indiscretions he chose to have. She searched for something to say to him, something to convince him to stay, but the words in her head were so scrambled she couldn't put them together to make any sense. She contemplated dropping to the floor, begging, crying, and pulling on his pants leg—anything to make him realize how much she loved him. Instead, she said nothing as she continued getting dressed.

With her coat draped over one arm, she sat down on the chaise. She clutched the straps of her purse and watched as Daron proceeded around the bedroom, collecting other personal items to pack.

"How long will you be gone?" she asked.

She practically whispered the question, afraid to hear the answer.

Christmas is already ruined. What next?

"I'll be back in mid-January," he replied without looking up from what he was doing.

Adrienne watched somberly as he tossed the items into the small carry-on that sat on the bed. He grabbed a couple of watches, a pair of cufflinks, and a pinky ring from the jewelry armoire and placed them in a brown leather jewelry case. Glancing at the clock on his nightstand, he picked up the pace and began quickly opening and closing drawers as he scurried about the room. After taking one final inventory of everything he had packed, he reached into the top drawer of his nightstand and pulled out his wedding band. Her head hung low as he slipped it on his finger; she realized she had not seen it since the day she ran into him at Target.

She intended to walk out with him so they could say their goodbyes at the side door. She would give him the most passionate kiss—the kind that would make him remember her even when he was with his wife. However, as he zipped up his carry-on, he turned to Adrienne in what was already an awkward moment.

"Uh, I don't need you to wait. I have a few phone calls to make," he said in a low voice.

He then walked over to her, leaned down, and gave her a light peck on the cheek.

"I'll call you when I get back."

Adrienne realized at that moment that Daron didn't plan to give her a gift for Christmas; it never crossed his mind to buy anything for her.

She fought to hold back the tears as she picked up her overnight bag from the floor. Feeling embarrassed along with many other emotions, she swung her bag and purse over her shoulder and darted out the room. As she ran down the stairs, she heard Daron's cell phone ring, and he answered it right away.

"Oh, hey, babe. I was just about to call you."

His voice grew faint as she landed on the bottom step and rushed down the hall. As she passed the doorway to the kitchen, she stopped short and then turned around. Without any reasonable thought, she walked into the kitchen and headed straight to the small cabinet drawer below the bulletin board that contained the sticky notes. She yanked the drawer open, then hesitated for several seconds. There was no plan nor an explanation for what she did next. She grabbed the set of keys labeled *HOUSE* out of the drawer before running through the laundry room and out the side door.

With the set of keys in her purse, she sped through the streets and arrived home in record time. She ran straight to her bedroom, ignoring her mother's sarcastic *"Hello. Glad you could join us"* routine, and locked her door. After placing her dirty clothes inside the hamper, she changed into a pair of sweats and got comfortable on the bed before fumbling inside the bag. Slowly pulling the keys from the inside change pocket, she held them in the air and stared. They were not just any keys. They were the *stolen* keys to the house of her married lover. Feeling a sense of panic, she looked around the room for a place to hide them until she could plan her next move.

Meanwhile, as Daron boarded his flight, he worried about his ongoing affair with Adrienne. *Have things gone too far?* He always had a great time with her, but she wasn't someone he would ever consider leaving his wife for no matter how bad things had been between them lately. After all, he and Linda had many years together and built so much between them.

124

Adrienne was still very young and naïve, although that was often what turned Daron on.

After settling into his first-class seat, Daron ordered a drink to calm his nerves. He was concerned about Adrienne's reaction. He thought maybe he had taken things too far with her but also wanted to make sure she would be okay. He promised himself to check on her when he could get a moment away from Linda.

Chapter Sixteen

Christmas in the Keys

Linda spent the entire weekend having the home in Key Largo decorated in a beautiful Christmas motif. It took all day to have the seven-foot spruce put up and decorated, the banisters trimmed with garland, and to guide the decorators on how to hang colorful lights around the roof so that they highlighted the house perfectly. Wanting everything to be ready, she stayed busy, shooing everyone around to meet her deadline. Linda knew how overwhelmed Daron had been at work, so she wanted to surprise him with everything instead of waiting to have him do it himself. She knew he would rather jump in the pool or spend time riding up the canal on his boat than unravel strings of Christmas lights.

When all was done, she looked around the house and was pleased with the outcome. It was five-thirty. Daron's flight would be arriving by seven, and she had just enough time to put the food in the oven. She was going to make this night special. It had been a while since they had been together, and she wanted to make it up to him.

Linda wasn't sure what had been happening between them lately but felt she was somehow losing Daron. Yes, she spent a lot of time promoting her latest book, but lately, he seemed pretty distant even though she thought she was making an effort to spend time with him. Sometimes it crossed her mind that maybe he was cheating. *God, I hate to say that word.*

The last time things were like this, Linda was spending many hours at the university. While Daron was building up his insurance business, she spent more than enough hours at the university trying to become the best, most impressive professor there was. She spent late nights in her office preparing notes for lectures, then brought ten-page term papers from her two classes home and spent hours in her home office combing through each report and meticulously grading them. She hadn't realized how much she was neglecting her husband until she came across the tube of lipstick in their car that they shared. At first, she figured some envious woman slipped it in the car to rile something between her and Daron. Many of his clients were single women as his insurance business grew. The advertisements for his company and business cards with his photo were everywhere. Handsome, charming, and successful, Daron's photo of him wearing a grey suit and burgundy tie while standing in front of his insurance agency was enough for any woman to try her shot at him. Linda wouldn't put anything past some of the women who practically banged on his door looking for insurance and then some.

When Linda found the lipstick, she first laughed it off and jokingly confronted Daron about which one of his lady friends slipped the tube into the side pocket of their car door. She expected the two of them to laugh it off until his facial expression told something different. That blank glare like a deer in headlights, followed by the tears swelling in his eyes, cut through her heart like a dagger. Daron put his head down, and Linda prayed that what he had to say would be part of the 'joke'.

"Babe, we have to talk," he started.

There was a long pause between them. She wasn't sure if

she wanted to hear what he had to say. She braced herself, not wanting to believe he had done the inevitable.

"What is it?"

She tilted her head down to try to make eye contact with Daron, but he continued without once looking up at her.

"There has been someone else. It's nothing serious; we've just been spending time together. I'm sorry."

That moment changed things in the worst way. After hearing the sordid details of Daron's affair with an old colleague he rekindled with through social media, Linda threw him out of their condo and immediately hired a divorce attorney. She was determined to end their marriage and had already calculated her half of the assets plus the condo.

Somehow after Daron's pitiful pleas to reconcile, Linda forgave him and took him back. However, there were conditions, and Daron promised to adhere to them, even if it included getting rid of his social media accounts and checking in with her several times a day.

"The only information I want to see about you online is on your company website. Get your business growing, not your social life."

Daron held his head down and humbly agreed. His accounts were deleted that night.

Linda knew what she was doing. Daron had yet to make his first million, but she knew it was coming. If they were to divorce and she got half (or everything), it still wouldn't be enough for her. Linda saw the potential in Daron's insurance company; there was much more room for growth. Daron was not only a people person with a charming personality, but he had great selling and business skills to build a million-dollar empire.

I'm not stupid, she thought.

That was years ago, and since then, the two had fallen in and out of love a hundred times. Yet, the money continued to move in the same direction—up.

Linda chuckled to herself as she reminisced about the time she wanted to leave Daron. They've built so much together through the years. She reminded herself that giving him another chance was the best that could have happened between them.

Yes, we're going to be just fine.

*****

Daron arrived in Key Largo late in the evening. As he pulled up to the house, he noticed the flickering colorful lights on the lawn and in the windows. *She decorated already.* He was surprised yet glad the decorations were already done. He walked into the house to the aroma of seafood. There was an array of lobster, scallops, and mussels in the kitchen, along with steamed vegetables and a couple of bottles of wine spread out on the table.

"Hey, baby, how was your trip?" Linda asked.

She was wearing a sexy, backless dress and a pair of high heels. Daron missed coming home to a good dinner and a sexy-looking woman. He dropped his bag and wrapped his arms around her.

"It wasn't too bad. Mmmm, I missed you."

"I missed you, too. I hope you're hungry."

After dinner, he jumped in the shower and then came downstairs to sit in the living room with Linda. They sat by the Christmas tree that flickered with colorful lights while the O'Jays belted out *Christmas Just Ain't Christmas Without the One You Love* through the music channel of the television hanging on the wall in front of them. They were both quiet; Linda seemed relaxed and content, while Daron was full of guilt and disgusted with himself. They sat for a couple of hours listening to music until they both drifted off to sleep.

By midnight, the couple dragged themselves to the bedroom and slid under the covers. Linda caressed Daron's chest before making her way down to his boxers. He was quite surprised and, although exhausted, began to perk up. *This is something new.*

As she continued to pleasure him, visions of Adrienne came to his mind, which he quickly dismissed. It had been barely twelve hours since lying in bed next to her, but it was now time to focus on his wife. He gently pulled Linda up towards him and flipped her on her back, then slid his head between her legs to reciprocate the pleasure. She moaned in ecstasy and grabbed his head, begging for more. Once she was satisfied, he entered her. At first, it was almost like a strange encounter because he had become so familiar with Adrienne. However, as he began to warm up to her, he became more acquainted with the woman he loved until he finally exploded inside her. At that moment, he knew this was what he lived for—this is his life, his love, and no one else. Adrienne was a fling. She was cute and something to fill a temporary void, but he had everything he needed right there with his wife.

He rolled over and drifted off to sleep. When he woke up, the sun was rising, and he could smell the coffee brewing downstairs.

Mmm, smells like my baby's down there cooking for me.

He got up to pee and brush his teeth, then threw on a pair of shorts. He opened the blinds to the bedroom window. It was already hot at 7:40 a.m. *I'll see if Linda wants to take a ride on the boat today.*

He walked downstairs, expecting her to be in the kitchen, but she wasn't there. The breakfast he smelled was on the counter, cold. A note was left on the table.

Hey, babe, help yourself to breakfast. I'm meeting up with Carol and Sandra. Will be out most of the day. Love you.

Daron dropped the note back on the table, but it fell to the floor. He didn't bother to pick it up. Instead, he poured a cup of coffee from the pot, which was still hot, then sneered as he eyed the plate of cold eggs, bacon, and toast sitting in front of the microwave. He didn't know if this was karma, but it would be a very long winter if this was anything close to what he could expect.

Chapter Seventeen

Uncontrollable Urges

Adrienne spent most of her days locked in her room, moping and crying over Daron while having time off for the holidays. She was angry and depressed by the unexpected news that Daron would be spending the holidays with his wife. *The nerve of him.* She felt alone, especially since no one knew the truth about her married lover.

Christmas was the gloomiest of days and could not end fast enough. Adrienne skipped the traditional breakfast with her mother and Kara and lay in her bed the entire morning. When her dad called to wish his girls a Merry Christmas, Adrienne claimed she wasn't feeling well and would talk to him another time. Uncle Jim, her mother's brother, and other family members came over for dinner late that afternoon. It took every bit of strength for Adrienne to get up and get dressed to make an appearance at the dinner table. She did her best to act like she was okay but felt miserable inside. All she could think about was Daron, wondering how he and Linda were spending their day and imagining Linda opening the gifts she thought were meant for her. She didn't have an appetite, so she excused herself after claiming to be sick.

It was twelve-thirty in the morning; she woke up realizing she had cried herself to sleep. The house was quiet except for the low sound of voices on the television in her mother's bedroom. As she lay on her bed staring at the ceiling, she thought about the humiliating experience that took place. She blamed Linda for it all, seeing her as the one thing standing between her and Daron.

Any attempt to get back to sleep was clouded with an overwhelming feeling of anger as she imagined Daron and Linda together while she lay in bed alone.

1:02 A.M.

After tossing and turning for several minutes, Adrienne sat up on the edge of the bed and stared into the darkness, contemplating. She felt the need to do something, anything but sit there in the quiet and dark. Reaching for her phone, she texted Daron, apologizing for leaving without a proper goodbye and telling him that she missed him. She sat on the side of the bed, waiting for him to respond. Twenty minutes later, there was still no response, which left Adrienne seething. Her mind told her that Daron was probably screwing his wife and had no time for her. *Bastard!*

She sat for a long time, going over everything in her mind. Adrienne had never felt so stupid in her life. Things were not going as planned. She had to do something. Finally, with the lights still off, she pulled out a pair of black sneakers and grabbed her black hoodie and sweats from the closet. After getting dressed, she retrieved the stolen keys from her hiding place and slowly opened her bedroom door. *It's time to take a ride.*

She paused in the hallway for a few seconds and listened for the rhythmic snoring that confirmed her mother was sound asleep. Closing her bedroom door behind her, she crept down the hall and made it to the front door. When she stepped outside, the freezing temperature immediately hit her in the face, and she ran to her car to escape it. Without allowing time for the car to warm up, she immediately took off down the street before anyone could notice. The road was empty except for a single vehicle passing in the opposite direction. Her heart raced as she sped through the streets, barely slowing down at stop signs and accelerating through yellow lights. She hadn't quite thought things through, but the impulsive moment exhilarated her and prevented any chance of her coming to her senses.

As she merged onto the Bronx River Parkway, heading south towards Scarsdale, she picked up speed. She couldn't wait to get to her destination. In about fifteen minutes, Adrienne found herself turning onto the private road. She turned off her headlights and drove down to the end of Daron's street. After making a U-turn, she slowly pulled up in front of the enormous Mediterranean home, where she stopped to get a better look. There were no lights on at the property, except for the outdoor lamps lighting the path to the front door. At first, she tried to reason with herself. *This is crazy. Go home.* Yet, instead of listening to the voice in her head, she headed back to the main road and drove about three-quarters of a mile until she reached a huge church. She quickly turned into the church parking lot and swung around the back where she parked in the dark.

After shutting off the engine, she reached into her front pocket and wrapped her hand around the keys. Just thinking about it gave her an adrenaline rush, and she swung the car door open and got out. As the cold winter air ripped through to her skin, she pulled the hood of her sweatshirt over her head. Using the mini flashlight from her keychain, she walked up the main street towards Daron's house. The road was empty and dark; the only sound she could hear was the occasional snap of a twig underneath her feet. Adrienne's fearlessness made her oblivious to the risk she was taking as she cut through the densely wooded lot that led directly to the back of Daron and Linda's house. She walked a few hundred feet before reaching the stucco wall surrounding the property. It was easy to climb over, and she squeezed through the tall, bushy evergreens that lined the wall before sprinting across the large, manicured lawn. The moon was bright, creating enough light for her to see a clear route to the back of the house. Adrienne slowed down and walked around the edge of the covered pool to the side door she was accustomed to entering. After jiggling one of the keys into the hole, she heard a clicking sound, indicating the door was unlocked.

In a few seconds, Adrienne was standing on the other side of the door. Pausing for a moment, she listened to the silence that filled the dark house. With the bright glimmer of her flashlight, she made her way through the laundry room and halted briefly to catch her breath. Her heart was beating so fast; she was both nervous and thrilled. She listened carefully for any signs of life and then took off her sneakers so as not to track any dirt from the woods into the house. Although there were no lights on, the moon brightly beamed through the windows, allowing her to see just enough as she slowly tiptoed her way through the house.

Feeling more at ease, Adrienne continued down the hall. She imagined herself living in the house as she walked through the darkness. *It was nice kicking it with the girls. Why are all the lights off? Oh, Daron must be upstairs asleep. My poor baby works so hard. I bet I know what I can do to wake him up.* Adrienne giggled at herself as she fantasized about her life with Daron.

With her hands lightly touching the walls to guide herself through the darkness, she made her way to the staircase and headed up to the master bedroom. Once inside, she scanned the room and reminisced about the last time she and Daron were there together. It was a painful reminder, but she assured herself that he would be back and everything would be okay.

Her fingertips gently brushed over the dresser as she made her way towards Daron's walk-in closet. Feeling secure enough, she turned on the light and scanned the walls of dress shirts, slacks, and sweaters neatly displayed on the shelves and racks. Recognizing one of her favorite sweaters Daron often wore, she pulled it off the shelf. His cologne still lingered on the cashmere pullover. Putting the sweater to her nose, she inhaled deeply, and it almost brought her to tears. She turned off the light and carried the sweater back to the king-sized bed, where she cradled it in her arms until she fell asleep.

The next morning, she jumped up in a panic after realizing she had slept through the night. Adrienne quickly folded the sweater and placed it back on the shelf before sneaking out the side door. The sun was slowly rising, and she needed to make sure she returned to her car before it was light enough for anyone to notice. Retracing her steps from the night before, she ran back to her car in the church parking lot and headed home.

Once in her own bed, she lay under the covers thinking about the thrilling events of the night before. It was comforting to be back in Daron's bed, even if he wasn't there. She giggled to herself at the thought of how easy it was to get inside their home.

*****

The rush Adrienne felt after sneaking inside Daron and Linda's house lingered for days afterwards. It was as if she had discovered a new way to be in Daron's life—roaming around his house and clinging to his personal belongings. To her, it was the next best thing to being with him, although it was a dangerous way of doing so. Her heart raced when she replayed her actions—hopping over the wall, creeping across the yard, and carefully making her way around the home as if she owned it. She would never have done such a thing had she not known Daron and Linda seldom used their alarm system. It was another issue Daron was frustrated about when it came to Linda. She often left the house without arming the alarm. She felt they lived in such an affluent neighborhood that it would be easy to recognize someone who didn't belong there. Besides, their good neighbors always looked after each other. Daron gave up fighting with Linda when arriving home often to find the alarm unarmed. He would let her learn her lesson when all her furs were stolen. In the meantime, he made sure his possessions were well-insured.

For the next few days, Adrienne walked around the house singing and whistling with a smile on her face.

"What's gotten into you?" asked Kara.

"Nothing, lil' sis. Just feeling good, that's all."

Adrienne's little secret kept her in a good mood for days, and she chuckled when she overheard Kara and her mother talking about her.

"She must be seeing that boyfriend of hers again, Mom," said Kara.

They were sitting in the living room watching a program while Adrienne stood in the kitchen doing the dishes.

"You're probably right, baby."

The mother and younger daughter giggled at their conclusion and continued about the mystery man in Adrienne's life. Meanwhile, Adrienne could only hope to be back with Daron again soon.

Chapter Eighteen
What Would Linda Wear?

Adrienne spent the next day and a half shopping for the perfect dress for Staci's New Year's Eve celebration. Knowing Daron was spending his time with Linda, she wasn't very motivated and agonized about what to say when she showed up at the party without him. As Adrienne browsed through several racks of dresses, she worried about facing her friends. How would she pull off Daron not showing up with her after all the talking she did about finally introducing him? She came up with several stories about why Daron couldn't make the event. *Something last-minute. Uncontrollable.* It would be an emergency, perhaps forcing him to leave town quickly. *That's it. I'll say he had an emergency in Florida.* Anything to save face. After all, her friends were expecting to meet her mystery man.

After several hours, she grew tired of shopping. Besides, it was almost closing time, and she was frustrated that she still hadn't found anything. Whatever she picked out was either well over her budget or unflattering when she tried it on. *What would Linda wear?*

Adrienne searched for something elegant and classy. She

thought of the many dresses Linda wore in the photos on the walls. Beautiful designer dresses enhanced her figure and looked as if they were made especially for her. From looking at her pictures, Adrienne could tell Linda put a lot of effort into selecting her wardrobe; the beautiful dresses, shoes, and accessories always looked perfect on her. Adrienne could only dream of having a wardrobe such as hers.

Just as quickly as the idea came to her, she instantly brushed it off. She laughed at the thought of her crazy suggestion and blamed it on not eating all day and having exhaustion from all the walking around. However, after leaving the eighth store without any success, Adrienne began considering her outlandish idea. *I must be crazy.*

Empty-handed, Adrienne left the mall with a feeling of desperation. As she drove through the congested streets, she found herself thinking more and more about her last option. She was in such deep thought that she barely remembered the drive home. By the time she arrived, Adrienne had her plan mapped out to perfection.

The next evening was New Year's Eve, and shortly after seven o'clock, her mother and Kara headed out for the evening church service. Adrienne had been pacing back and forth in her room and was relieved the moment she heard the front door close and the sound of her mother's car driving away. That's when she threw on her coat and gloves and jumped into her car.

The adrenaline rush was almost unbearable as she sped through the dark streets and onto the ramp leading to the Bronx River Parkway. With visions of the many designer dresses floating in her head, she couldn't wait to get inside Linda's closet to review her options. It had occurred to her that she was about to commit a crime, but she dismissed any thoughts of wrongdoing as she pulled into the parking lot behind the church.

After sneaking into the house and up to the master bedroom,

she turned on the light in Linda's walk-in closet. It almost angered her to see the beautiful array of high-end clothing Adrienne knew she could not afford. There she stood in front of the rows of couture dresses and gowns in every style and color she could imagine. She slowly brushed over the collection of satins and silks with trembling hands while shaking her head in amazement. She had never seen so many high-end labels in her life: *Givenchy, St. Johns, Escada, Chanel, Valentino, Gucci, Prada.* Designers she had only seen in magazines filled the large closet that was practically the size of Adrienne's bedroom.

After carefully examining the wardrobe, she pulled out a black Oscar de la Renta cocktail dress that caught her eye. The dress had a plunging scalloped V neckline and three-quarter laced sleeves. The wide waistband flared into a short, silk bubble skirt that hung inches above the knee. She noticed it still had a price tag on it as she ran her fingers over the material. It was the perfect cocktail dress for the evening.

Within seconds, her jeans and sweatshirt were on the floor, and she slipped the dress over her head. Adrienne modeled the dress, looking at her reflection in the tri-fold mirror. Her slim yet curvy five-foot-seven frame filled the dress perfectly, and Adrienne was convinced the dress was made just for her. On the opposite wall was a five-tiered shelf lined with various designer shoes. She picked out a pair of black three-inch stilettos and slid them on.

We wear the same size!

She walked over to the large jewelry armoire, where she pulled out a pair of black drop earrings and a matching necklace. As she turned to leave, Adrienne noticed a shelf in the corner holding several clutches and shoulder bags. Realizing she had been in the house too long, she quickly selected a small, silver, sequined box clutch. She didn't bother to look at the designer because she knew it cost more than whatever she had at home. Satisfied with her inventory,

Adrienne placed the jewelry in the clutch and hung the dress over her arm.

As she began to descend the stairs, she stopped short and contemplated. Adrienne remembered wandering through one of the rooms the last time she slept over. Inside was a climate-controlled closet with a glass door. At first, Adrienne didn't understand its purpose—until she went home and looked it up on the internet. *A cooler for clothes?* Now that she remembered, she couldn't stop herself from the temptation of trying one on. She ran back up the steps to the spare bedroom and opened the door to the special closet. Her eyes widened at the sight of them.

There are so many!

She hastily scanned the closet to make her choice.

Opting for the full-length, she pulled the dark mink coat off its rack and headed back down the stairs. For a short moment, she hesitated, thinking maybe she was taking things too far. However, as quickly as those thoughts came to mind, she quickly brushed them off.

*****

Adrienne was dressed and ready to go to the party in no time. Her hair was pinned in an updo to show off the black drop earrings, and the matching necklace fit perfectly. She felt like a confident, beautiful woman in the nearly five-thousand-dollar dress and couldn't stop admiring herself in the mirror.

By ten o'clock, she headed for the door. This time, Adrienne knew she couldn't avoid her mother. She and Kara had already returned from church. They were sitting in the living room eating popcorn and watching television as Adrienne passed by.

"Nice dress. Where'd you get that?" her mother asked.

She sat up on the couch to get a better look and eyed Adrienne up and down.

"This? Oh, I had it for a while. It's old."

"Old? It looks expensive. I hope you didn't blow all your money on—"

"Don't worry, Mom," she interrupted. "I got a good deal."

Adrienne leaned over to kiss her on the cheek. Then turned to Kara and kissed her on the cheek, as well, before heading out.

Before getting into the car, she opened the trunk and pulled out the mink. She knew she had a good chance of getting away with wearing the dress in front of her mother, but there was no way to lie about a fur coat.

In less than ten minutes, she was parked a block away from Staci's house. The street was lined with cars as Adrienne followed the path leading to the brightly-lit estate. She held her head high as she briskly strutted to catch up with a group of guests who were dressed in clothing just as expensive-looking as hers. She entered the large vestibule, and one of Staci's hired assistants greeted her and the other guests with glasses of champagne. Another welcomed Adrienne and offered to take her coat just as Staci entered the hallway. Staci took one look at the coat, and her mouth dropped open.

"Where did you get that?" she asked.

Adrienne was so excited about her new outfit that she had forgotten to put a story together about where she got the mink coat.

"It's my mom's," she replied in a low voice. "Just something old I found in her closet."

"Oh my God, girl. I thought maybe you stole it or something," she said, followed by a loud chuckle.

Staci did a double-take, then her eyes widened after noticing Adrienne's dress.

"By the way, I love that dress! You're looking classy tonight. Is this the dress Daron bought? By the way, where is he?"

Staci looked behind her for Daron to appear.

Adrienne thanked her and laughed nervously without

answering her question as she followed Staci into the living room. Inside the room stood crowds of people laughing and chatting while they sipped from their glasses and nibbled on hors d'oeuvres passed around on silver platters. Holiday music with a jazzy beat piped through the speakers in the ceiling. Adrienne wondered if any of Staci's wealthy friends would notice her expensive dress. In the past, when Adrienne showed up at Staci's events, she would shy away from the ritzy crowds. This time, she walked through the room as if she were one of them.

Jacki was already there, along with her new boyfriend, Mason. Adrienne joined them on one of the couches as they sipped on champagne.

"Where's Daron? I thought you were bringing him?" Jacki asked.

Staci, who was still standing over them, waited for a response. She had her hand on her hip as if she would not leave without an answer.

"He had to leave town this morning. There was an emergency at his home in Florida."

Although fully prepared to share the story she came up with about Daron's emergency, Adrienne hoped her friends wouldn't spend too much time focusing on him. She was already saddened that he would rather be in Florida with Linda than spend the holiday with her. Talking about him would only remind her of that.

"Oh, he has a home in Florida?" Jacki asked.

"Well, couldn't he have someone down there take care of it? I mean, it's New Year's Eve. Who does that?"

"Are you sure this guy isn't married? He's been M-I-A since you've first mentioned him," Staci asked with a chuckle.

Adrienne felt cornered with all the questions. *Does Staci know the truth?* Adrienne knew how much Staci loved to google people, and she was beginning to worry she had already done some research on Daron. Staci gave Adrienne a serious look, then burst out laughing.

"I'm just kidding with you…but you tell him we *demand* that we meet him soon."

Adrienne exhaled as Staci walked away to tend to her other guests.

"Girl, I love your dress," said Jacki. "Is that the dress Daron bought you?"

Adrienne braced herself and prepared to enter another story of lies.

"Uh, yes, he bought it for me when we went shopping at Saks."

Jacki shifted in her seat and leaned over to get a closer look. She raised her eyebrows and gently touched Adrienne's sleeve with her fingers.

"It's beautiful. He's a keeper. You'd better not let this one go."

Jacki clung to Mason's arm, who sat quietly as he indulged in the small plate of hors d'oeuvres sitting on his lap.

"Don't worry. I won't," Adrienne replied while trying to remember if she had hidden the price tag.

*****

Although she couldn't show off Daron at the party, she was satisfied her story about him was convincing and even more thrilled everyone was impressed with her wardrobe. Adrienne left the party shortly after everyone toasted to the New Year and headed back to Daron and Linda's house. She had a duffle bag already in her car packed with her regular clothes, and after parking behind the church, she changed into them and headed towards the house. After letting herself in through the side door, Adrienne realized how oddly comfortable she felt sneaking in and out of the house. It *was* odd, and although the thought of getting caught sometimes crossed her mind, the thrill of having access to the house whenever she wanted overpowered her cautions.

After taking her time carefully putting everything back in its place, Adrienne retraced her steps to double-check that she hadn't left anything out of order. It was 2:15 a.m., and she knew nothing would be happening between now and daylight. So, she decided to roam around the house a little longer. Using the flashlight from her keychain, Adrienne took her time getting a closer look into the couple's lives. She started pulling out dresser drawers and inspecting the items inside. Linda's drawers were full of lacey underwear, bras, fancy sweaters, and silk blouses.

With all of this, what more could she possibly have in Florida?

Then she moved to Daron's side, and as she began searching through Daron's drawers, she carefully picked up his folded t-shirts and boxers and held them close to her chest. A soft, powdery laundry scent clung to his underwear and reminded her of the good times she had with him. She selected a pair of navy-blue boxers because she knew blue was his favorite color and stuffed them in the pocket of her jeans, then left the house with the cherished garment.

It would only be a couple more weeks before Daron's return, and she fantasized about the two of them seeing each other for the first time since December.

He'll call me as soon as his plane lands to tell me to meet him at his house. When I arrive, he'll greet me at the side door with a big hug and kiss. He'll hold on so tight that I'll barely be able to breathe. When he lets go, he'll plead with me to forgive him for running to Florida to Linda. I'll forgive him, and he'll lead me up the stairs to the bedroom. He'll make love to me all night. The next morning as we are sitting in bed eating breakfast, we'll discuss how he'll break the news to Linda that he is madly in love with me.

Adrienne convinced herself that if she concentrated on the way she wanted things to happen, it would happen just that way. So excited, she barely made it through the next two weeks before he returned. On the night before she expected him to return, she lay in bed too excited to sleep. The next day, she took off from work to get her hair and nails done. She wore one of his favorite outfits and anxiously paced around the house while waiting for his call. By five o'clock, there still was no word from Daron, so she decided to call him.

The phone went to voicemail several times, and Adrienne began to worry.

Maybe I should drive by to see if he's home.

She was becoming frustrated. By now, they should have been in each other's arms, softly whispering how much they missed each other while tearing off each other's clothes.

Finally, after midnight, Daron answered her call.

"Hello?" he said in a subdued voice.

"Hey, babe. I've been worried about you. Are you back in New York?"

"Hey, Adrienne. Uh, yes, I got back a couple of hours ago."

Daron didn't sound like his usual self, and Adrienne noticed right away.

"Well, when can we get together? I missed you so much."

There was a long pause on the phone, and Adrienne immediately became concerned. *Had he spent so much time in Florida with Linda that he no longer feels the same?* Before giving him a chance to respond, Adrienne jumped in.

"I know it's late, so how about we meet somewhere when you get off tomorrow? Is that okay?"

"Yes," he responded. "Let's meet about six o'clock in the parking lot by Neiman's."

His response was far from what Adrienne expected. *Why aren't we meeting at his house?* She reluctantly agreed to meet in the garage and decided not to inquire further about it. She was just happy to be able to see him again finally.

*****

Adrienne was so excited about seeing Daron that she could barely get her work done the following day. Even Mr. Fredericks noticed how distracted she was and raised his eyebrows when she didn't respond to his requests fast enough.

When the day was finally over, Adrienne went to freshen up her makeup in the restroom. She wore a winter-white pantsuit that fit snugly around her curvy hips. The low-cut blouse showed just enough for a tease. She knew it would be something Daron would love on her, and although something about meeting him made her nervous, she hoped he would still find her irresistible.

She sped through town and pulled into the mall garage, driving up several ramps before pulling next to the black Escalade. Unlike the other times they met, Daron remained in the front seat.

"Hey," she said as she kissed him on the cheek.

She expected a passionate kiss in return, but Daron stiffened up as she leaned towards him.

"What's wrong?"

Why aren't you in the backseat? She at least expected the usual backseat routine; however, seeing Daron fully clothed sitting behind the steering wheel alarmed her.

"Adrienne, I have to tell you something," Daron began.

He looked straight ahead, and the serious tone of his voice let her know he was about to say something she didn't want to hear. She took a deep breath, then turned her body to face him.

The words coming from his mouth were garbled. Not because he wasn't speaking clearly, but because Adrienne just couldn't bear to hear them. He was breaking up with her. Spending time in Florida with his wife helped him realize that what they were doing was wrong. He loved his wife very much, and this "thing" needed to end.

Many other words were coming from his mouth, but Adrienne couldn't hear anything else by that point. His muffled voice began to fade away as he went on and on about love, marriage, vows, etcetera, etcetera.

Adrienne sat in silence, staring into space. She felt Daron's hand lift her hand as he placed a soft kiss on her wrist.

"I wish you all the best," was the last thing she heard.

"How did you let her change your mind about me?" Adrienne asked him.

She was trying to control her anger. They had something special, and Daron was being led by his selfish wife.

"What? I don't know what you mean," Daron responded, shocked by Adrienne's question.

"You were making love to me the whole time she was gone, and now you think you're going to discard me on her say so?" Adrienne asked him.

She was looking for Daron to explain this to her in a way she could understand.

"Adrienne, you knew I was married from the beginning. I never lied to you." Daron reminded her.

"And you know I'm in love with you and have been from the beginning. What am I supposed to do now, Daron?"

At this point, Adrienne was starting to tremble; she was so hurt and angry. Daron was seeing a side to Adrienne he didn't know existed and one he didn't want to deal with. He had to take control of this, or it could spiral out of control.

"Look, you knew what this was—it was about two people making each other feel good. Nothing more, nothing less."

He had to bottom line this and cut Adrienne short. She could be a problem, and he couldn't and wouldn't let that happen.

"Oh, that's all I was to you? A piece of tail? You got me messed all the way up!" Adrienne shouted.

"You need to get out, *now*," Daron said as calmly as he could.

Adrienne continued to rant and rave, trying to get Daron to see her side. Daron sat listening, thinking she would leave once she had her say. However, her tirade was never-ending, and Daron couldn't listen to it anymore.

"Adrienne, get out," he said, reaching over her thighs to open the door.

Nothing could have hurt her more. Daron dismissed her like she was a common whore in the street. Adrienne stared at him with tears in her eyes before she turned and got out of his vehicle. Daron watched as she walked to her car. It tore him apart that he had to speak to her in the way he did, but he had to control this situation.

She didn't remember the drive home nor passing her mother and Kara as she walked directly to her bedroom. It was as if her world had suddenly come to an end.

How could this happen?

Her heart ached as she tried to think of what she could have done wrong. She didn't understand the concept of marriage— that the bond between Daron and Linda was much stronger than the short-lived fling between them. All she saw was the fact that the man she loved was suddenly taken away from her, and the pain was more than unbearable.

Linda.

Her hurt turned into anger as the image of his wife floated in her head.

There was a light knock on the door, followed by the muffled sound of Kara's voice. She asked Adrienne if she would like to see her new dress for her winter social. Without responding, Adrienne turned off the lamp on her nightstand and lay on her bed until she cried herself to sleep.

Chapter Nineteen
Call It Women's Intuition

D aron and Linda's marriage had always been full of ups and downs—even this last trip to Florida. Although Linda planned to make it enjoyable for Daron by welcoming him with beautiful holiday decor and a delicious dinner, she fell short when she disappeared the next day, leaving Daron all alone. Daron was so angry about it that he considered getting on the next flight back to New York, but somehow, Linda managed to smooth things out, and Daron decided to give things another chance. The two decided to sit down and have a serious talk, and finally, Linda was ready to listen. Daron didn't know why, but suddenly, she had a change of heart.

"Babe, I want you to know how much you mean to me. I'm willing to do whatever it takes to keep this marriage together. If it means spending more time at home to be with you, then that's what I'll do."

Daron heard the words he had wanted to hear for the past several years. Now maybe he would get his wife back. He was tired of the last-minute trips, him coming home to an empty house, cold food left for him on the counter, waking next to an empty side of the bed, and text messages saying goodbye. He wanted them to go back to the way they were when they were first married—having fun, laughing, spontaneous lovemaking in crazy places, all the things he had with Adrienne.

They spent the rest of the trip rekindling, bonding, and enjoying themselves amongst friends and entertaining guests like the happily married couple they used to be. When it was time for Daron to return to New York, he and Linda spent a quiet evening together by the pool. While the two cuddled, they sat in silence, yet the communication was clear. There had been a mutual understanding between them, and both were willing to work on fulfilling the other's needs. Plans were discussed about their future—things meant for both and not leaving one of them home and lonely. They were falling in love again, and nothing or no one would come between them.

The following day, Linda saw Daron off at the airport. The two embraced and said their goodbyes at the gate. Daron boarded the plane looking forward to a new start for their marriage and was excited about Linda's decision to cut her stay short and return to New York two weeks later. Although the two discussed the issues they had been having in the marriage, Daron didn't dare divulge his affair with Adrienne. After Linda threatened him with divorce the last time she found out he had cheated, Daron knew she wouldn't give him another chance. Besides, the business had grown into an empire since then. Now Linda would get half of everything, and the thought of giving up half of what he worked so hard to build made Daron angry just thinking about it.

If she wanted to know, wouldn't she have asked? Daron quickly dismissed the guilty feeling about not telling Linda. *Some things are better left unsaid.* He was just happy he and his wife had a mutual understanding and were willing to compromise to make things better. Now all he needed to do was break the news to Adrienne.

*****

Two weeks later, Linda was on her way back to New York. As she boarded the plane, she wasn't her usual chipper self. She held her head down as she entered first-class, avoiding eye contact with anyone on board. She had shortened her winter stay in Florida this year so she could spend more time with Daron back home. It was her way of fulfilling her part to maintain a healthy marriage by not being apart from him for months at a time. She hated the winters in New York but decided she'd rather endure the cold than lose her husband.

As she buckled her safety belt, the flight attendant greeted her and offered her a selection of drinks. Linda ordered a glass of white wine, then unfolded her blanket and laid it across her lap. She inserted her headphones in her ears and turned the volume up. She wanted to tune out all the thoughts she had in her mind.

Although they never talked about it, she was sure Daron was cheating on her again. She had yet to find solid evidence, but his behavior seemed off lately. The thought of him cheating angered her. Yes, she knew she'd been selfishly engrossed with her work and traveling, even when she didn't need to be, but how dare he even think about someone else!

I mean, I'm enough for him!

She took a large sip of wine and dismissed the vision of her husband lying beside another woman.

Ha! She laughed aloud. *You do you, and I'll keep doing me!*

She took another sip of wine, then lay her head back on the cushion of the headrest and focused on the music. As the flight took off, she closed her eyes and tapped her foot to the beat, letting any negative thoughts fade into the rhythmic sounds until she drifted off to sleep. However, it was only a matter of time before her mind raced with angst, and doubts about her husband's fidelity began to cloud her head. *Stranger in My House* by Tamia played from her old-school playlist.

Len Richelle

How appropriate, she thought.

However, now she couldn't tell who the stranger in the house was—Daron or herself. She suddenly opened her eyes and stared straight ahead at the seat in front of her.

Chapter Twenty

Meet Lauren Lash

Linda was poised, beautiful, educated, and successful. It was no wonder why Daron would have fallen for her. She was fifteen years older than Adrienne, a world traveler, and an established professor and author, while Adrienne, young, naïve, and fresh out of college, still lived at home with her mother and sister. Adrienne sat in her room making mental notes as she compared herself to Linda.

What will it take to win him over?

Then it hit her. Maybe if Daron saw the same qualities in her that he saw in Linda, he would become more attracted to Adrienne and run back to her.

I will have to be just like her and then some.

It sounded crazy, but for Adrienne, it meant winning Daron back.

She started by looking at Linda's social media pages, including her author website, *Meet Lauren Lash*. As an author, Linda always promoted her books, so Adrienne set up an account under a fictitious name and followed her like a loyal fan. Every day, she checked her page to see what was happening in Linda's life. Most of the time, Linda posted positive, inspirational quotes and announced the dates and locations of her book signing events. She posted pictures of herself with colleagues attending special events at the university where she taught. On occasion, she shared posts about personal events like birthdays and graduations of family members. Seldom did she post anything specific about Daron, but he was always standing by her side in the photos.

One morning, she posted an announcement about an upcoming book signing. She was scheduled to appear at a bookstore nearby on the following Saturday to promote her latest novel. Seeing this as an opportunity, Adrienne sat up in her bed to re-read the details of the announcement. Several ideas ran through her head, making her heart palpitate with excitement.

Should I go? I'll finally get to meet her. Will Daron be there? I should tell her everything.

Adrienne copied down the information and considered her next move. She was still hurting from Daron's breakup and desperately wanted him back. She hated Linda and blamed her for her current heartbreak.

She hated Daron and believed he deserved to be hurt, too, yet loved him enough to keep pursuing him. It wasn't long before she made up her mind. It was time to have a face-to-face meeting with her lover's wife.

I'll tell her about Daron and me. I'll make a grand entrance and interrupt everything.

Adrienne stood up from the bed and looked in the mirror. With her hand on her hip, she smirked at her reflection, proud of her wicked idea.

Everyone will hear what I have to say when I tell her the truth about Daron and me. I'll let her know all about her husband's nasty little habits. It'll leave her with her mouth wide open.

Excited about her plan to humiliate Linda, Adrienne took the time to prepare for her surprise debut. She selected a stunning, blue tight-fitting dress that fell perfectly over her curves and a pair of three-inch heels. The dress wasn't from a high-end designer like the ones Linda wore, but Adrienne felt empowered the moment she slipped it on.

The week seemed to take longer to come to an end. Finally, on Saturday morning, Adrienne woke up early to shower, dress, and make sure everything was perfect. She made a special trip to the M.A.C. counter to have her makeup done before driving to West Nyack to the Palisades Center Mall bookstore.

When she arrived, she scanned the parking lot and almost immediately spotted the red Tesla Model X that belonged to Linda. Nervous yet excited, Adrienne proceeded into the store and headed towards a table to her right that displayed the latest collection of new books. One of them had a picture of a woman running through a field. Adrienne noticed the author's name in bold letters: *Lauren Lash*. Positioned next to the table of books was an easel with a large poster board headshot of Linda. She was smiling while posing with the same book in her hand. Printed at the bottom of the poster were the details of her book signing: *Today from 12 - 2 p.m.*

Adrienne grabbed one of the books from the display table and paid for it at the register before heading back to the far-left corner of the store. When she arrived, about fifteen people were standing in line waiting for their turn to meet Lauren Lash. As Adrienne joined the line, she could see a woman sitting at the table up front greeting fans and signing books. *It's her.*

There she was in the flesh: Lauren Lash, aka Linda. The sight of her made Adrienne's heart flutter. Linda was more beautiful than her pictures, donning a tan pantsuit, lavender button-down blouse, and lavish accessories to match. Linda smiled as she sat at the oblong table holding a shiny gold pen in her hand, ready to sign at her fans' requests.

Adrienne gazed as Linda greeted each fan and made small

talk while penning personal messages on the blank pages inside their books. Occasionally, she would let out a courteous laugh when someone tried to impress her by quoting particular scenes from pages in the book. The crowd within earshot laughed along as they admired their favorite author sitting in front of them. From what Adrienne could see, Linda was pleasant, sociable, and a well-admired individual. Adrienne scoffed. She was no match for Linda. Adrienne could never imagine seeing herself in front of a crowd of people waiting to see her. She'd probably cower under the table if she knew so many people were eyeing her. She wasn't the social butterfly like Linda, nor did she believe she could ever be.

They all love her.

Adrienne's insecurities haunted her, despite the makeup, new hairdo, and dress that no longer made her feel empowered. Even her new nail polish started to chip, and she quickly made a fist in disgust to hide it. *Now what am I gonna do?*

The further she moved up the line, the better she could see how flawless Linda was. The jealousy started to creep up on her, and any doubts about her plan disappeared. *She needs to know.*

Her stomach was in a ball of knots as she decided it was time to tell Linda the ugly truth about her husband. In her head, she practiced the words while watching Linda enjoy her happy life.

Hi, I'm Adrienne, and I think you should know I've been sleeping with your husband. Hi, I'm Adrienne, and I think you should know I've been sleeping with your husband. Hi, I'm Adrienne, and I think you should know I've been sleeping with your husband. Hi, I'm—

"Next, please," said a woman standing next to Linda's table.

Adrienne assumed the woman was Linda's assistant. She stood over Linda while controlling the line and took photos of fans who graciously posed holding their newly purchased books with their favorite author standing by their side.

Adrienne walked to the front of the table, stood directly in front of Linda, and nervously handed her the book. There she was, face-to-face with her lover's wife.

"Hello," Adrienne whispered.

She put on a bashful grin and stared in awe at the beautiful woman sitting in front of her. *So, this is Linda.*

Linda took the book and greeted her with a radiant smile.

"Hello, is this book for you?" asked Linda.

Adrienne gently shook her head yes. Still, she could not take her eyes off Linda.

"Okay, what is your name?" Linda asked, holding the gold pen in hand, preparing to write.

"Adrienne. A-D-R-I-E-N-N-E," Adrienne replied.

Her voice softened even more as she cited the last three letters of her name. Linda tilted her head and strained to hear Adrienne speak, then began scribbling something inside.

As she watched her pen words in beautiful cursive writing, Adrienne quickly dismissed the idea of exposing the truth about her and Daron. She studied Linda's flawless skin, perfectly coifed hair, and stylish outfit. She had a beautiful smile with pearly white teeth and long, freshly manicured nails with wrists adorned with beautiful white gold bangles that sparkled so brightly. Linda was perfect.

No wonder he chose her over me.

When Linda handed Adrienne the book, Adrienne couldn't help but notice the diamond ring and wedding band on her finger. Linda thanked her for her purchase, and Adrienne quickly headed out the door.

Once in the car, Adrienne condemned herself for not having the nerve to follow through with the plan. Linda intimidated her, and Adrienne knew there was no way she could compete with all she had. *Unless she knows the truth.* She sat in her car a few minutes more to debate on whether or not to march back into the bookstore and tell it all. After all, it was what she had come for and what she thought might be the last resort to get

Len Richelle

Daron back.

Adrienne sunk in her seat and sighed. It was too late. She'd look crazy to go back inside, and she regretted not doing what she intended to do. After a few minutes of stewing over her botched plan, she opened the book and read the written message.

To Adrienne,
Thanks for your support. I hope you enjoy the book!
XO, Lauren Lash

Adrienne had no idea what the book was about, so she flipped to the next page and continued reading. It should have been expected but caught her by surprise.

For my loving husband, Daron: Thank you for always being there.

Adrienne slammed the book shut before reading any further and started the car.

When she arrived home, her mother and Kara were in the kitchen having lunch. Adrienne ignored her mother's questions about why she was dressed up so early on a Saturday and headed to her room. She tossed the book towards the dresser, and it fell to the floor. Without bothering to pick it up, she quickly pulled off her dress and put on a pair of sweats. She stepped over the book and lay across the bed to sulk.

After a brief nap, she woke up to find the book sitting on the dresser. Her mother must have passed by the room and seen it on the floor. Adrienne had no intentions of reading it, but she picked it up from the dresser and scanned through the pages. Linda's 250-page book was a fictional novel with an inspirational message about a woman who overcame trials and tribulations in her life.

How typical.

After taking a second look at the back cover, Adrienne decided to read a few pages, expecting to tear it apart and criticize every word. However, she found the story to be upbeat, inspirational, even humorous and found herself reading until the late hours of the evening. She had to admit it was a great book, and Lauren Lash, or Linda, was actually a great writer.

Adrienne carried the book around in her tote and read it every chance she got. If work was slow, she pulled out the book, and she couldn't wait to get home to curl up on the bed and read some more. In just a few days, she was finished reading but felt as if she had not gotten enough. She searched online and ordered another one from her collection. It was a tough four days waiting for it to arrive, but as soon as it did, she locked herself in her room until she read it from cover to cover.

Chapter Twenty-One
Guess Who's Coming for Dinner?

"Where have you been, girl? What's been going on?" asked Staci after Adrienne finally returned her phone call from several weeks ago.

"Oh, I've been busy, mostly with work," she lied.

"Well, I was hoping we could all get together before I go away on vacation."

"Vacation? Where are you going?" Adrienne asked.

"I thought I told you already. Anthony is taking me to Cabo for my birthday," she responded.

Time had flown by so fast, she forgot about Staci's birthday. *It's this weekend.* Adrienne scanned through her calendar on her cellphone.

"Oh, that's right. It's this Sunday. Okay, let's get together this weekend before you go," she replied.

Birthdays for the three of them were always something they made sure to celebrate together. When they were younger, they gave each other surprise parties in their backyards or the basement of their homes. They would make gifts for each other in art class at school, and their mothers would help them bake cupcakes and cookies. Now, as adults, they still found a way to spend time together.

After hanging up with Staci, Adrienne called Jacki and discussed Staci's birthday plans.

"Staci's paying for dinner? Why? It's her birthday," Jacki asked.

"Because she wants to have dinner at that restaurant on the top floor of the Ritz. Who else can afford to pay for dinner there except her?" Adrienne replied.

The restaurant at the top of the hotel was one of the classiest restaurants in town and had panoramic views of the entire city. It was one of the places Daron mentioned a few times, and Adrienne imagined Daron someday taking her there for dinner. At least now, she would have a chance to see the upscale restaurant, albeit without him.

For Staci, money was not an issue, and she didn't mind treating her two best friends to dinner at the five-star restaurant, even if it was her birthday. The reservations were made for six o'clock, and Jacki drove them there. Several large dinner parties were already seated and celebrating their own occasions when they arrived.

"This must be the weekend to celebrate," Jacki said as they walked through the restaurant towards their table.

Floral bouquets and gift bags topped several tables throughout the dining area. Seated across from their table was a large party that appeared to be celebrating a wedding anniversary. Adrienne sat with her back facing the table belonging to the large party, while Staci and Jacki sat across from her.

Immediately after they were seated, the server greeted them and provided drink menus. They ordered a few cocktails and made a toast in honor of Staci. While waiting for the main course, they munched on fried calamari and shrimp cocktails.

Adrienne was having a great time and realized how much she missed hanging out with her friends. Since childhood, they had shared everything with each other. That is why it bothered her that she could not share her affair with them. As a married woman, Staci would definitely not approve, and Jacki, who had in some form or fashion probably already learned her lesson about married men, would tell her not to waste her time.

The large party seated behind Adrienne was full of laughter and seemed to be having a good time. The servers kept coming with bottles of champagne and large platters of food.

"That looks like a nice couple," Jacki said as she observed the neighboring party enjoying themselves, her words beginning to slur as she sipped on her third drink.

"Yes, I'm so happy for them. Marriage is a wonderful thing," added Staci, then clasped her hands and glanced at the wedding band on her finger.

"Oh, look, they're about to make a toast. Ooh, he's fine, girl. Look at him. I'll take him when she gets done," Jacki said.

She turned the glass up to her mouth but realized it was empty. As their server passed by, she motioned for him and asked for another drink. Staci scoffed at Jacki, then turned to Adrienne.

"I guess one of us will be the designated driver."

When Jacki's fourth drink came out, she lifted her glass while one of the guests at the neighboring table proposed a toast. She elbowed Staci to get her attention.

"Look, now the husband's giving a speech," Jacki said.

She and Staci focused on the table behind Adrienne, who laughed at the two taking so much interest in the group of strangers. Realizing the two of them were both inebriated, she decided to humor them and act as if she, too, were interested in the strange couple's anniversary dinner. She pushed back her chair and turned around to toast with the table behind her. The large dinner party held up their glasses as the handsome husband stood at the head of the table and began his speech to his wife, who was sitting down next to him.

At first, Adrienne thought her drink must have clouded her vision because the man making the toast looked exactly like

Daron. Then when she looked down at the woman to who he was professing his love, she recognized Linda in a beautiful red dress, dabbing the tears from her eyes with a white linen napkin. Adrienne looked at Daron again, and her heart sank as he looked into Linda's eyes while mouthing the words, *I love you.*

The group clinked their fluted glasses with one another and took sips of their champagne. Adrienne stared at Daron as he gulped his drink, smiled at his wife, and then leaned down to kiss her on the lips while the guests at the table applauded. He took his seat and then took another sip from his glass. Suddenly, he caught sight of Adrienne and nearly choked on the champagne in his mouth. He squinted his eyes, then after confirming it was Adrienne, he glared at her for a few seconds. The color disappeared from his face, and his lovely smile turned to scorn. He quickly looked away and gulped down the rest of the champagne before nervously hanging his head down.

Daron had been clear and firm when he broke it off with Adrienne. He chided himself now for being stupid enough to become involved with her. The notes she had written in the street should have told him that Adrienne wasn't all the way there mentally. How the hell was he going to get out of this?

Adrienne stared at him, unable to move and shocked at the sight of him. Feeling a combination of hurt, jealousy, embarrassment, and sadness, she watched him calmly wipe his upper lip with his napkin and quickly shake himself off as he joined in the conversation with the others at the table. His wife had no idea her husband's ex-lover was just a few feet away as they celebrated their tenth wedding anniversary.

Adrienne suddenly felt a knot in her stomach and wanted to leave. She knew it would break her best friend's heart if she just bolted out the door in tears, but there was no way she could last a minute longer with Daron and his wife seated right behind her.

"I think the calamari and shrimp are getting me sick," she announced.

"Really? Do you feel nauseous?" asked Staci, who was still munching on the few bits of calamari left on her plate.

"Yes. I can't take it anymore. I'm sorry. I think I'm going to have to leave."

Both Staci and Jacki looked at each other with confused expressions on their faces, then looked back at Adrienne.

Jacki took a sip of her apple martini.

"You were fine a minute ago. You must have eaten a bad shrimp. Let's call the waiter and let him know they're serving us bad food."

"No, no, don't bother." Adrienne stood up and placed her napkin on the table. "It could've been something I ate earlier. I'm sorry, Staci."

With tears in her eyes, she looked at Staci, who didn't bother trying to hide the look of disappointment on her face.

Adrienne pushed in her chair and walked over to hug her. As she leaned into Staci, Jacki grabbed her wrist and pleaded for her to stay.

"Why don't you go into the bathroom and put some cold water on your face? It might help you feel better."

Ignoring Jacki's suggestion, Adrienne reached over to hug her and then quickly pulled away. At this point, nothing would make her stay.

"I'll make it up to you. I'm so sorry," she said, then turned to leave.

She rushed past the large dinner party without looking in their direction and headed out the door. Once she reached the lobby, she realized she had ridden there with Jacki. So, Adrienne called for a Lyft to pick her up at the mall across the street. She didn't want to wait in front of the hotel in case Daron or any of his guests came out behind her.

As soon as she arrived home, she went straight to her room. Her mother heard her coming in and stopped in the doorway.

"That was an early night," she commented.

She watched Adrienne toss her dress in the corner of her closet and stood there waiting for an explanation.

"I don't feel well," Adrienne finally said.

She didn't look up from what she was doing. She just wanted to be alone, and if she talked any longer, the tears would come rushing out. Them celebrating their anniversary only validated that their marriage was still going strong.

After seeing that Adrienne was in no mood for small talk, her mother walked back into the living room and continued watching her program. Adrienne's cell phone rang a few times; she saw it was Staci and Jacki calling but decided to ignore them. She was too emotional to talk to anyone and felt horrible about walking out on her best friend's birthday.

I'll deal with them in the morning.

*****

Daron took a sip of the champagne and donned a fake smile, then lifted his glass and took another huge gulp. He looked around the room for their server. He needed to drink something much stronger than the weak champagne being passed around.

What the hell is she doing here? He couldn't help but wonder if Adrienne had followed him to the restaurant. Surely, she can't afford to dine in a restaurant such as this. She knew it was a place he and his wife had eaten at a few times before. *Would she really do that?* Daron stewed over the thought until Linda, somewhat tipsy, leaned on his shoulder.

"This is so nice, babe," she whispered in his ear.

She gently bit the tip of his earlobe and turned back to the other guests at the table. Daron focused on the bubbles floating in Linda's champagne glass. He was afraid to look up for fear of seeing Adrienne approaching the table. All he could imagine was her and her posse walking up to the table, ambushing him in front of everyone. Poor Linda would be hurt and

168

embarrassed. Hell, he would be embarrassed for her.

"Are you okay, babe?" Linda asked.

He snapped out of his trance and nodded yes. Linda turned away and continued talking to the guests at the table. Now his fear was turning to anger.

How dare she come up in here interrupting our anniversary dinner.

All he could do was be on alert, waiting for Adrienne to make a scene. It would be a chaotic one, but he would play it off.

I'll act like I don't even know her crazy ass.

He reached for his empty glass, then grabbed Linda's that was half full. After taking a gulp from her glass, he took a deep breath before looking back at the table. However, when he looked for Adrienne, all he saw was an empty chair. He looked around and even looked behind him to make sure she hadn't snuck up behind him.

Maybe she went to the restroom.

The other two young ladies continued to eat and talk. Daron then noticed the plate setting was gone, and the area had been cleaned.

She's gone.

"Babe, they're bringing out the cake," said Linda as she grabbed his arm and leaned in closer to him.

The waiter approached the table carrying a two-tiered cake with lit sparklers on top.

All at once, their guests shouted, "Happy Anniversary!"

Chapter Twenty-Two
Hashtag Burberry

The next morning, Adrienne called Staci to apologize. Lucky for Adrienne, Staci was pretty hungover and wasn't up to asking many questions like she normally would. She graciously hurried off the phone after wishing Staci well on her trip to Mexico. Next, she called Jacki and gave her the same story, although Jacki didn't let her off the hook as easily. Adrienne had to do more to convince Jacki that she was sick.

"I was throwing up so much when I got home that my mom almost called 911," Adrienne told her.

Jacki must've fallen for her story because she offered to pick up something from the drugstore and drop it off for Adrienne.

"Oh no, thank you. Mom got everything I need. In fact, the medication I just took is starting to make me drowsy. I think I'm going to take a nap now. Maybe we can meet up later."

Adrienne had no intentions of meeting with Jacki, though. If Jacki agreed to meet with her, Adrienne would think of an excuse not to see her.

"Oh, I can't. I was getting ready to tell you that Nate surprised me when I got home last night. He's taking me to

Atlantic City later. I'm packing as we speak," Jacki said.

Adrienne suddenly felt a knot in her stomach. She was happy for Jacki yet felt sorry for herself. First, it was Staci going away with her husband, and now Jacki was going away with her newest boyfriend.

They haven't even been together that long, and he's already taking her on trips.

"Oh, that sounds great. I hope you have a good time," she said before hanging up.

Suddenly, Adrienne felt alone. Everyone around her seemed to be happy and with someone except her. Even Kara was starting to go out on dates with a boy from high school.

Sitting upright against her fluffed pillows, she began scrolling through her social media sites. Staci had already posted pictures of the birthday dinner from the night before. There were several pictures of Staci and Jacki showing off their food and drinks, and even the two of them posing with the restaurant staff as they sang "Happy Birthday" with Staci's birthday dessert in front of them. Adrienne appeared in only one photo—the one taken in front of the fountain in the lobby when they first arrived. She wished she hadn't left so abruptly and knew it was not very mature of her, especially since it was Staci's birthday dinner.

They just wouldn't understand.

After looking through all the photos of the evening's events, she logged on with her fake account, only to find pictures of Linda and Daron enjoying their celebration.

Happy Anniversary to Us! There were several pictures of Daron and Linda in the restaurant, posing with their guests around the large table. Adrienne's heart sunk. She still could not believe she ended up at the same restaurant and a table right next to Daron and his wife.

As she continued to scroll through the photos, she came across one message that piqued her interest:

Next stop, Paris! #Happyanniversary.

Adrienne smirked at the idea that the two would spend the next nine days in romantic Paris. She grabbed her computer and frantically began to search for flights. Adrienne knew she couldn't pull the same stunt she did when she flew to Florida.

*****

Monday morning, Adrienne woke with feelings of anxiety. She could not help but wonder how the couple was spending their time in Paris. She picked up her phone to check Linda's page, only to discover several pictures of Daron and Linda posing in front of the Eiffel Tower, Champ-Élysées, and Arc de Triomphe.

Adrienne tossed the phone down and buried her head in her pillow. Tears of frustration dampened the pillowcase as she lay on her side and stared at the wall. It should have been her with Daron. She had to make him see that they were meant to be together. Seeing pictures of Linda and Daron together was slowly becoming Adrienne's undoing.

She lay there for the next thirty minutes while imagining herself with Daron. *It has to happen soon.* She envisioned their lives together, living in the Mediterranean-styled house and taking trips together to romantic places such as Paris. Doing all the things Daron was now doing with Linda.

During her fantasizing, Adrienne thought of an idea. It was risky, but as she plotted the details in her head, it became more and more appealing. She waited for her mother to leave for work and Kara to go off to school before initiating her plan. Next, she called Mr. Fredericks to inform him that she would not be in that day.

"My tooth has been aching all weekend. Yes, I'm contacting my dentist as soon as the office opens."

Then she picked out a pair of shorts and a t-shirt to put over her bathing suit. *It's time for a new swimsuit*, she mentally noted.

By the time she left the house, the temperature had already reached ninety degrees, and the humidity made it feel ten degrees hotter. She blasted the A/C in her car as she headed south on the Bronx River Parkway. Her plan had her feeling nervous, but she put on her sunglasses and turned the volume up on the radio to tune out her thoughts. *Besides, they're out of the country.*

After pulling into the church parking lot, she took a deep breath and thought for a moment. She was close to talking herself out of her plan. After all, it was broad daylight. However, she quickly dismissed her fear and rationalized that she had reason to continue.

Everyone else is having a great vacation. Why shouldn't I?

After grabbing her beach bag, she casually strolled three-quarters of a mile down the road towards the house, then cut through the densely wooded lot. The brush was thicker now than in the summer, and Adrienne regretted wearing her new sandals instead of something more comfortable.

When she reached the perimeter wall, she tossed her bag over the other side, then carefully climbed over and pushed her way through the bushy evergreens. She let herself in the house through the side door and continued through to the main part of the house. It was her first time being back inside the house since Linda's return from the Keys.

As she crept slowly from room to room, she noticed a few changes around the house. Overall, the place seemed fresher and brighter, with a new area rug in the foyer, a couple of brightly-colored paintings on the walls, and a few new potted plants in Linda's office. Adrienne also noticed a floral scent in the air that reminded her of freshly-washed laundry.

She has definitely added a woman's touch.

After inspecting the entire first floor, Adrienne crept upstairs and headed straight to the master bedroom. The bed had a new floral-print duvet with matching shams covering the king-sized pillows. Linda's dresser had a few more bottles of perfume than the last time Adrienne was there, and on the chaise were a couple of opened gift boxes that she assumed were gifts for their anniversary.

Adrienne walked into Linda's custom-built closet for a quick peek at the many designer dresses and shoes that she knew she could never afford. She brushed her hands against the expensive fabrics that hung on the racks, carefully pulling out the new ones she had not yet seen. One dress stood out, and she became excited the moment she spotted it.

The red dress.

Adrienne pulled it off the rack and examined its intricate details. It was the red satin cocktail dress with spaghetti straps that Linda wore for the anniversary dinner. She looked at the tag and gasped. *Dolce and Gabbana.* Adrienne wanted to try it on so badly but decided to save it for another time. She was on another mission for the day.

After rummaging around the closet a few minutes more, Adrienne opened one of the drawers to find a collection of bathing suits and cover-ups. She spotted a two-piece Burberry bathing suit inside. She picked it up and admired it as she contemplated. It was her size, and she knew it would look perfect for photos. Quickly tearing off the old one-piece she was wearing, Adrienne replaced it with the bikini. After modeling it in the mirror, she let down her ponytail and applied a little gloss on her lips. Satisfied with her look, she gathered her belongings.

Before heading back downstairs, she glanced at the doorway of Daron's closet. She had no interest in going inside. Her curiosity about Linda had overpowered her desire for Daron in a very strange way. Adrienne shrugged her shoulders and continued down the stairs.

Since no one was home, there was no need to tiptoe around. Adrienne was comfortable as she made her way through the halls, pretending it was her home. She unlocked the patio door and stepped outside. The sweltering heat immediately hit her in the face as the sun beamed down from the sky. Standing on the patio, she took her time to view the entire yard, admiring its peacefulness and tranquility. She laid her beach towel across one of the lounge chairs and walked over to the pool. While holding on to the metal railing, she eased her way into the cool water. When she adjusted to the water's temperature, she completely immersed herself into the pool and swam to the other side.

After a few laps, Adrienne lay on the lounge chair to dry off in the sun. She didn't give a second thought to breaking into her ex-lover's home and dozed off for several minutes. When she became hungry, she helped herself to the snacks she found in the pantry. She found a margarita mix and helped herself to a cocktail as she stretched out by the pool. Adrienne took a moment to scroll through her phone to see what everyone else was up to. Jacki had posted several pictures of her and her boyfriend by the beach and inside one of the casinos. Adrienne smiled at the picture of her friend holding up a martini glass to toast to those who weren't there with her.

Staci posted photos of her and her husband in Mexico and commented about the great time she was having for her birthday. There were several pictures of her enjoying the beach and showing off as she floated around in the water.

By her third margarita, Adrienne was oblivious to her surroundings as she began taking selfies with her phone. *After all, I look good in this Burberry.* At first, she posed lying on her back in the chair. Then she took a few of her in the pool. She took several more shots with the house in the background, then took another twenty minutes to crop, delete, and adjust the color so that they were perfect enough for posting. After taking another sip of her margarita, Adrienne pressed the send button with a caption included.

Having fun in the sun! #Burberry.

Immediately after uploading the photos, she realized what she had done.

What if the wrong person sees them?

In a panic, Adrienne attempted to delete the photos, but already she had received a text message from Staci.

Where are you? That place is fabulous!

Adrienne hesitated before texting back. She knew each lie she told would only lead to no good.

His house.

OMG, fabulous! Better meet him soon. Looks like a keeper!

Will do.

After sending the text, Adrienne started receiving several notifications on her phone. Friends began commenting on her photos and telling Adrienne how beautiful she looked in her bathing suit. Comments such as *Nice Burberry, Looking good, Nice place,* and *Lucky you* flooded her page, and Adrienne had second thoughts about deleting the pictures.

She enjoyed all of the compliments and could barely keep up with them as she responded with *Thank you* and a heart to each one. It was the first time since Daron that she had gotten so much attention, and she was having a ball.

Suddenly something came over her.

"I shouldn't be here," she said aloud.

She took one last gulp of her margarita, then gathered up her things to go inside. After changing back into her clothes, Adrienne rinsed out the bikini and tossed it into the dryer, then folded it and placed it back inside the drawer. She carefully went through the house to straighten up whatever she had moved and ensured she hadn't left anything out of place.

After taking one last look to admire the beautiful home, she exited through the side door and sadly headed back to her small room at her mother's. Adrienne told herself that she had to get a grip. Going in and out of Daron's house was crazy, and she knew it. But for some reason, she couldn't stop herself.

*****

Len Richelle

When Jacki and Staci returned from their trips, all three ladies met up at Staci's house. Adrienne knew she would be bombarded with questions about her poolside pictures, so she spent some time rehearsing what to say.

"Why didn't you take pictures of the two of you? We don't even know what he looks like," Jacki asked.

"I'm not ready to reveal him to the public," Adrienne answered.

Jacki nodded as if she understood; however, Staci began to pry deeper.

"Are you sure he isn't married?" Staci asked.

Adrienne felt her face turn red.

"No, he's *not* married," she snapped, glaring at Staci.

Adrienne hated her for always wanting to know more than she was ready to reveal. Staci looked back at Adrienne and saw the anger in her eyes. She realized she had gone too far with questioning Adrienne.

"Oh, sorry," she said, holding her hands up as if to surrender. "I'm just wondering why we haven't met the guy yet."

"In due time," Adrienne responded, then looked away, hoping she had finally put an end to Staci's questioning.

Adrienne was sure of one thing. She was tired of all the lies. Daron was living his life as if Adrienne had never been in it. She had to do something; she couldn't let it go on this way.

Adrienne knew she was taking a calculated risk, but enough was enough. She had been calling Daron, but he refused to take her calls. It had been months since that awful night in his car when he told her he didn't want to see her anymore. Adrienne had thought Daron would change his mind about them, but he didn't. Now, she had become angry. She thought Daron owed her something. She did give him her body willingly, which he was more than willing to take. Now, he wanted to treat her like she never existed, like he never ran his tongue along the column of her neck, like he had never kissed her inner thigh, or like he never called her name when he thumped inside her body. No, she wouldn't be discarded like trash. Daron would give her the respect she deserved, and she knew just how to get it.

Adrienne had planned everything to the last detail as she drove to Daron's office. She would tell him what she had to say, and he would listen. Today she would have her say.

She pulled into the parking lot, finding a space. Then she took a deep breath, turned off the ignition, and got out of her car. She had picked just the right outfit and shoes. Adrienne wanted Daron to see what he had been missing.

Adrienne pulled the door open, walking through it.

"May I help you?" the receptionist asked with a smile.

"I'm here to see, Daron Weathers," Adrienne responded, stopping at the front desk.

Her mind was telling herself to turn around and leave. This was not going to end well, but she couldn't stop herself.

"Do you have an appointment?" the young woman asked, flipping through the page of appointments.

"No, I don't," Adrienne answered, growing impatient.

This woman was slowing her down. She had worked herself into a full head of steam on her drive there, and Adrienne didn't want to lose her momentum.

"Call him on the phone and tell him he has a guest," Adrienne ordered, leaving the desk and heading to Daron's office.

"Wait! You can't just go to his office," the receptionist called out as she watched the back of Adrienne make her way down the hallway.

The young woman did what Adrienne told her to do; she picked up the phone and called Daron. Adrienne walked through her old department, not speaking to anyone. There were murmurs, and her former co-workers pointed as they talked about her. Adrienne didn't care what they said; she was on a mission.

Len Richelle

Daron had taken the call from his receptionist but had no idea who could be coming to see him. He stood buttoning his suit coat. Just about the time he moved around his desk, the door opened, and Adrienne walked in, closing it behind her. The shock on Daron's face and the fact that he couldn't speak told Adrienne that she had made the right decision to show up unannounced.

"You and I need to talk," Adrienne said, stopping in front of his desk.

"What the hell are you doing here, Adrienne?" Daron asked, finding his tongue.

He had to get her out of his office and quick.

"Did you think you would just screw me and never speak to me again? You can't throw me away that easily, Daron," she said, dropping her purse in one chair and taking a seat in the other.

"Adrienne, you can't be here," Daron replied nervously.

He didn't know what Adrienne would do. He had to be careful; he didn't want to set her off. The objective was to get her out of his office as quickly as possible.

"I've been calling you, and you won't take my calls," she continued, ignoring him,

"We don't have anything to talk about. It's over, Adrienne. I'm sorry, but it is what it is," he said, moving to take his seat behind his desk.

He thought putting space between them was a good idea, but there was nothing that could save him from Adrienne's wrath. She stood, and putting her hands on his desk, she leaned forward. Daron watched her face change into someone he didn't recognize.

"Who the fuck do you think you're fucking with? I'm not to be played with, motherfucker!"

Adrienne didn't recognize her own voice. It was like she was standing outside herself, telling herself to leave—that this was wrong. Daron had been straight with her from the

180

beginning. What did she expect him to do? The whole thing was crazy.

Daron lost his breath as he listened to Adrienne flip on him. The more she talked, the louder she got. Daron realized he had to get her out of there before the whole building would be privy to his affair. He was thankful Paula was on vacation. Daron pushed out of his seat, quickly moving around his desk to grab Adrienne by her arm.

"Get the hell out of here! How dare you come in here acting a damn fool in my place of business! You knew what this was; I never professed undying love for your ass!" Daron yelled as he ushered Adrienne to his private entrance.

Adrienne tried to wrestle out of Daron's grip, but she was no match for his strength. Daron grabbed her purse as he dragged her to the door. Adrienne continued to yell the whole way.

"Get the fuck outta here! If you come back here, I'll have your ass arrested. Do you hear me?!" he said, opening the door.

By now, someone was knocking at the door and calling Daron's name—asking if everything was alright. Daron didn't respond.

"I'll tell your wife," Adrienne threatened in a last-ditch effort to get his attention.

Daron snatched her close enough that she felt his breath on her face. "You go anywhere near my wife, and I'll choke your fucking tongue out," he said evenly.

His tone was deadly, and Adrienne knew he meant every word he said. Daron opened a door leading to the parking lot, and he shoved Adrienne out the exit, throwing her purse behind her. He watched as it hit the pavement.

"I'm sorry, Daron. I'm so sorry," she said, realizing she had made a terrible mistake—one she knew she couldn't take back.

She started crying while Daron pulled the door shut. He never responded to her apology.

Chapter Twenty-Three
Lost in This Masquerade

Adrienne spent the rest of summer closely watching Daron and Linda's every move, although most of her focus was on Linda. Between following them around town as they ran errands and attended appointments to keeping up with Linda's social media pages several times a day, she would sometimes spend her entire day watching them. Well known within the community, it was obvious everyone admired the couple. Whenever they pulled up in front of a ritzy venue or restaurant, they would be greeted like celebrities and then escorted inside as a valet drove off with one of their fancy cars to park it in a special lot. Adrienne eyed them from afar as they carried on without any idea they were being watched.

Soon Adrienne began to take an interest in some of the things Linda did and got herself involved with similar activities. She was willing to try anything, especially if she thought it would help get Daron back.

"Since when did you start playing tennis?" her mother asked.

It was a Saturday morning, and Adrienne was heading out to a group tennis lesson. She was wearing a new tennis outfit and carrying her new Babolat Pure Drive tennis racquet. She had the racquet custom-made after seeing Linda post about the one she recently purchased.

"Just trying out new things," Adrienne said as she exited the front door.

Tennis was just one of many things she became interested in after watching Linda through the fence of the tennis club where she was a member.

With every penny she made, Adrienne began upgrading her wardrobe. While she always wore the latest fashions, she started dressing up more often, no matter where she was going. One weekend, Jacki was having a birthday party for Carson, her five-year-old son. When Adrienne showed up, Jackie was annoyed to see her at the door wearing a white, two-piece pantsuit and high heels, similar to the one Linda wore at her book signing.

"Where do you think you're going?" Jacki asked.

She stood in the doorway with her hands on her hips as she looked Adrienne up and down. A bunch of five-year-old kids was screaming and running around in the background.

"What are you talking about?" Adrienne asked as she pushed her way past Jacki and walked through the door.

Spider-Man decorations and red balloons filled the house. Some parents were sitting around in the kitchen while others watched their children play in the bounce house in the backyard. Adrienne knew she was overdressed but didn't care.

They'll just have to get used to the new me.

Adrienne said hello to the other women in the house, many of whom also looked her up and down as she greeted them. It was apparent they were wondering if she knew she was attending a child's birthday party, but Adrienne ignored their sneers and continued through to the backyard.

"Hi, Auntie Adrienne," yelled Jacki's son, Carson, as he ran up to her with open arms.

"Hello, my little munchkin."

Adrienne grabbed him and kissed him on the cheek while trying to avoid getting dirt on her white suit, then reached into her large white leather Marc Jacobs bag and handed Carson his gift. He screamed with delight when he unwrapped the small, remote-controlled helicopter she had bought him.

Staci arrived about twenty minutes later. After saying hello to everyone and giving Carson his gift, she immediately started questioning Adrienne.

"So, where are you going all dressed up?"

Adrienne was now starting to feel self-conscious. Usually, when she visited Jacki, she had no problems sitting on the floor with Carson to play or often ran around the house with him. Today, she was dressed as if she were going to one of Daron and Linda's high-society functions instead.

"Daron and I are attending an affair later. In fact, I have to meet him in a few minutes," she said, looking at her watch.

"We still haven't met him," Jacki responded with a frustrated look. She had her arms crossed and tapped her foot as if she planned to stand there until he showed up.

"Well, he's been busy," Adrienne snapped.

She stayed for another thirty minutes and watched the children play as she tried to mingle with some of the mothers. Then she announced that she had to meet her boyfriend to attend an event. Adrienne said her goodbyes and sighed with relief as she headed to her car. While driving away, she thought about how she was still pretending she and Daron were together. To her, it was starting to become a task. *Maybe I should just say we broke up.* That way, she wouldn't have to put on such a charade while trying to make up stories about him. She didn't know then how much deeper it would get.

Her fascination with Linda and Daron grew into such an overwhelming obsession that it began to consume her life. Most of the time, she focused on Linda and covertly followed her around town as she attended her engagements. Once, she drove an hour and a half away to a town in New Jersey and posted herself down the street for five hours while Linda visited relatives. Adrienne did almost anything just to get a glimpse of her. And somehow, her stalking went unnoticed.

On another occasion, Adrienne learned there was an open house event for a new gallery that Linda was attending. Linda posted the information about the event on her social media pages, encouraging everyone to come out and support a few local artists. Immediately, Adrienne signed up for the event and played out scenarios in her head about how the evening would be.

On the night of the open house, Adrienne dressed in a floral-print silk blouse and light-colored pants with a pair of high heels. As she finished up her makeup, the doorbell rang. She overheard her mother's voice welcoming the visitor and was surprised when Staci appeared at her door.

"I was just stopping by to see my friend who never calls," Staci said as she stood in the doorway of Adrienne's bedroom.

Arms folded across her chest, she walked inside and made herself comfortable on the bed. She scanned the room and then noticed Adrienne's clothing and makeup.

"Going somewhere?" Staci asked.

"Yes, I have an engagement," said Adrienne.

She continued to apply more lipstick on top of the coat she had already applied. Staci's presence made her uncomfortable because she knew how much Staci liked to investigate things.

"Oh, with Daron?" asked Staci.

Adrienne knew Staci was only trying to test her, but she was not going to let her win.

"Daron and I broke up. A while ago. I told you that."

Adrienne continued looking in the mirror without blinking an eye as she brushed a few strands of hair into place. Then she reached for the mascara and applied another coat to avoid turning to look at Staci.

"I'm going to an art gallery. Alone," she added.

"Oh, the one on Martine? I heard about the open house

tonight. Some new displays by local artists. Do you mind if I take a ride with you?"

Adrienne paused for a moment. She glanced at Staci's reflection in the mirror. This was a solo mission, and Staci would just be in the way. *On second thought, I could use the moral support. What if Daron shows up, too?* She would just make sure Staci didn't know anything about her real plans. She'd ruin everything for her.

"Sure, I guess. Let's go," Adrienne replied.

Then she grabbed her purse and headed out the room, leaving Staci still sitting on the bed. She looked back at Staci, who suddenly jumped up to follow her.

"By the way, you're driving."

On the way to the gallery, Staci talked on and on about everything from her family life, shopping for new shoes, and planning a surprise birthday dinner for her husband.

"I'm glad you invited me. We needed to catch up!"

Adrienne rode in silence as she stared out the window. She barely heard a word Staci said as the chance of seeing Linda danced in her head. When they pulled into the lot, Staci turned off the car and turned to Adrienne.

"What's gotten into you? You seem so distant," she asked.

"Nothing. I'm just busy with a lot of things, that's all," said Adrienne.

"Come on, Adrienne. I know you. Since when do you like going to art galleries? Is he going to be here? Daron? Is that why we're here?" Staci glared at Adrienne and would not budge until she got her answer.

No, but his wife will be, and I can't stop following her.

Adrienne wanted desperately to tell Staci the truth, but she knew Staci would not take it very well.

Looking straight ahead at the windshield, Adrienne calmly responded, "I'm just trying to do a few different things in my life, and that's *all*. I have nothing to do with Daron anymore, so please *never* mention him ever *again*."

With that, Staci nodded her head to agree, and they headed into the gallery.

Adrienne anxiously scanned the room, looking for Linda. She wanted to find her quickly so she could prepare herself in case Daron was with her. She couldn't handle another surprise like the one she had before.

The room was vast and full of large colorful prints of awkward-looking shapes and portraits of weird-looking people and animals. The crowd of people gathered around the oddly artful displays and appeared to be engrossed with them. Adrienne was relieved she brought Staci with her. She would not have felt comfortable standing at a painting pretending to admire it or like she understood it while praising the artist she knew nothing about.

Servers walked around carrying trays that held glasses of wine while others had trays of crackers and cheese. Setup in one corner of the room, a deejay bopped his head to the techno music he played for the crowd. Staci grabbed a glass of wine and tapped Adrienne's arm to follow her to one side of the room. She appeared to be more interested in the artwork than Adrienne and began taking down names of the artists of her favorite pieces.

After about fifteen minutes of walking around the gallery, Adrienne finally spotted Linda across the room. Adrienne was ecstatic and tried hard to contain herself so no one would notice. As usual, Linda was dressed beautifully and looked as radiant as ever.

"I'm going to look at some pieces over there I think I might like," she said, pointing across the room.

"Oh, you don't want to finish looking at this side with me?"

"I'm just going to take a quick look, then meet you back here."

Not giving Staci any time for debate, Adrienne quickly disappeared. Staci, who was enjoying herself anyway, went back to studying the display in front of her.

Adrienne nervously walked across the room where Linda was standing. She casually walked up behind her and stood close enough to inhale her patchouli-scented perfume yet distant enough not to be noticed. Linda was wearing a white linen two-piece and dangly fresh-water pearl earrings. Her hair was pinned up with a rhinestone clip, leaving a few strands loose to hang down her neck. Adrienne unobtrusively admired her as she stood looking at a large piece of artwork with her hands clasped in front of her. Another woman accompanied her, and both seemed drawn to the painting. It was a simple piece of artwork—a large butterfly with iridescent hues of purple, lavender, and pink surrounded by a wheat-colored meadow. For some reason, Linda was very intrigued with the painting and could not stop appreciating it. Adrienne overheard her tell her friend how much she loved butterflies and was very interested in purchasing the artwork. She raved about the vibrant colors that stood out against the pale beige background and how she commended the artist's brilliant talent. Then she turned to her friend and joyfully announced that she knew the perfect place to hang it.

"I'm going to hang it on the wall in my home office," Linda said with delight.

Overhearing the conversation, Adrienne looked at the painting and was reminded of Linda's color scheme in her office. The painting would perfectly match her throw pillows on the white loveseat. She was so absorbed with Linda and the conversation that she accidentally blurted out her thoughts.

"Yes, it would look perfect in there!"

Linda's smile immediately disappeared as she looked over her shoulder at Adrienne.

"Excuse me?" she asked.

Adrienne panicked as she quickly thought of a way to recover.

"I–I have a similar painting in my own home office," she stuttered.

She quickly turned around to leave and prayed Linda didn't recognize her. As she walked away, she heard Linda's friend ask if she knew her.

Terrified of being recognized by Linda, Adrienne made a beeline to the nearest exit door and proceeded out into the night air. It was a close call for her, and she leaned up against the brick building to catch her breath.

Oh God, I hope she didn't recognize me.

As she walked through the parking lot, she remembered Staci had driven. Adrienne sent a text message to Staci, indicating she was outside waiting and ready to leave, and Staci immediately responded.

What? I'm not done! I just met one of the artists!

Adrienne now realized it had been a mistake to allow Staci to come along. She had opened herself up for more questions that she didn't want to answer. Feeling the need to get away from the gallery as quickly as possible, Adrienne walked up the street and called for a Lyft. In five minutes, the car arrived, and she was headed home. That night, she got an earful from Staci, who told her how crazy she was for leaving the way she did. Quick to produce a defense, Adrienne managed to fabricate a story.

"He was there, Staci. I think he's been following me lately. I had to get out of there, fast."

Adrienne pretended to be distraught as she explained how her ex-boyfriend suddenly showed up at the gallery and how she managed to escape out the side door before he saw her.

"Oh my God, I'm sorry," Staci said. "I didn't know things were that bad with you."

Adrienne continued with her act as Staci listened empathetically. She even suggested filing a report and getting a restraining order. Adrienne assured Staci that if an incident like that happened again, she would go straight to the police. When they hung up the phone, Adrienne immediately felt the guilt of lying to her friend.

Now she thinks I have a stalker, when the truth is I'm the one doing the stalking.

*****

"This was great. Thanks for inviting me for a much-needed night out, Linda," said Raquel.

It was rare that the longtime friends got together anymore. So, Raquel jumped at the chance when Linda called to invite her to the gallery. She missed going on outings with her friend, and this evening gave them time to catch up.

"Of course, girl. I missed you."

The two stood in the parking lot and gave each other hugs as they said goodbye.

"I can't wait to have the painting delivered," said Linda.

She unlocked the car door and hugged her friend one last time.

"Tell Daron I said hello, and we've all got to get together some time soon."

"Will do," Linda told her. "Give my regards to Charles."

Linda was so excited about the new painting she purchased that she dialed Daron's cell before starting the car. It automatically went to voicemail. *Why isn't he picking up?*

She pulled out of the lot and began making plans to put up the new painting. She considered shopping for a few butterfly-themed trinkets that would complement the artwork and have Daron paint one wall in her office to match the colors in the painting. She couldn't wait until they had company so she could show off her new purchase. She would boast about the up-and-coming artist she supported by buying one of her expensive art pieces.

After arriving home, she went straight to her office and took down the old painting. There was nothing wrong with it. She had just grown tired of the dreary yellows and browns and wanted to brighten up the room.

Len Richelle

After placing the old painting in the garage, Linda kicked off her shoes and went into the family room. There was a time when she and Daron spent many evenings there—drinking, listening to music, and eventually tearing each other's clothes off before taking it upstairs to the bedroom. Now she couldn't remember the last time they were in that same space together. Linda wished he was there at that moment, even if only to enjoy a glass of wine with her.

She poured herself a glass of Riesling from the small refrigerator behind the bar, then flipped the switch that lit the fireplace. Before sitting down on the couch, she turned out the lights. The flickering flames already emitted enough light.

"Hey, Alexa. Play some smooth jazz," she said.

She closed her eyes and hummed to George Benson's "This Masquerade" as it resonated through the speakers in the ceiling. The song's words reached out to Linda as if George was singing a message directly to her.

As she sipped on her wine, she thought about the young lady who spoke to her at the gallery. She had a familiar face, but Linda couldn't remember where she had seen her before. Assuming she was in her early twenties, she could have been one of her students from her Creative Writing classes. However, Linda had an eerie feeling about her, and as she sipped her wine, she thought long and hard about their encounter.

She chuckled at herself as she took another sip of wine. She was just being paranoid. There was nothing to be concerned about with the young lady at the gallery.

I'm sure she's just one of my fans.

Chapter Twenty-Four

Big Brother

A drienne just happened to spot the black Escalade as she zoomed down North Avenue. She left work late one night, and on her way home, she cruised through the busy New Rochelle streets looking for a place to order takeout. As she slowly moved through the traffic, the shiny black Escalade parked on the left side of the street caught her eye. Immediately, she slammed on her brakes and leaned out the window, straining for a view of the license plate. She had made out the last three digits when the car behind her blew the horn to keep moving. Adrienne turned down the next street, then went around the block a second time.

Where would he be?

She looked around while slowly driving down the busy street. After circling the block for a third time, Adrienne found a parking spot around the corner from Daron's truck. She got out of her car, then carefully eased down North Avenue, scanning the stores and restaurants for any sighting of Daron. Suddenly, she spotted him inside the sports bar, almost directly in front of where his truck was parked. He was sitting on a barstool near the window, holding a tall glass of beer. Several people were inside; however, he directed his attention to a gentleman sitting next to him. The two appeared to be engaged in a serious conversation. The other gentleman's facial expressions indicated he disapproved of whatever Daron was telling him. Daron sipped his beer, then motioned the bartender for two more glasses.

Adrienne studied the two men from outside, oblivious to the crowds of people passing her. Daron never looked in her direction but continued talking to the man beside him. She tried to imagine what the conversation was about.

Maybe he's trying to decide between Linda or me.

Although she couldn't see the other man's face, she could tell he was about the same size and complexion as Daron. Then it dawned on her. *His brother, Derek.* Daron mentioned his older brother on occasion. He was the one who used to keep Daron in line when they were growing up.

She watched for about forty-five minutes before the two men paid their tabs and stood up to leave. Adrienne bolted back around the corner when they turned towards the door to avoid being seen by Daron. She cleverly peeked from the side of the building as Daron and his brother said their goodbyes. The two men embraced, then Daron hopped in his truck while his brother walked towards a car parked further down the street. Adrienne came from around the corner and stood in the entranceway of a building just a few doors down from the sports bar. She was careful not to get too close so Daron would not see her. He sat there for about five more minutes before driving off into the night.

*****

It had been months since Daron and Derek had spoken. When Derek flew out to New York for a business trip, he made sure he and his younger brother got together, even if only for a brief night out. The last time they spoke, Daron confided in him about his affair with Adrienne, and his older brother did not hold back his feelings.

"Man, what's up with you? Are you kidding me?" Derek said from the other end of the phone.

His voice was loud, and the choice words he had for his brother were piercing to Daron's ears.

"You know that's nothing but trouble, bro. Linda would skin you alive, then take all your money."

Daron gave his older brother several reasons to justify his affair with the sexy young beauty he'd been seeing, but Derek was not so understanding and abruptly interrupted.

"End it. Right away. Before all hell breaks loose and you lose everything."

Now that Derek was in town for a few days, he wanted to check up on his brother and make sure he was doing the right thing. They met up at the sports bar near Daron's job. After catching up on family business, there was a long pause between the two as they sipped on their beers. Daron knew it was coming and braced himself for the lecture.

"So, have you had any run-ins with that young lady since we last talked?"

Daron gulped his beer, and a flashback of Adrienne at the restaurant during the anniversary dinner came to his mind. Derek and his wife had attended the dinner; however, Daron never revealed that Adrienne showed up. He still wasn't sure whether she had done it on purpose and thought it was best not to make it an issue at the moment. Nor did he want to tell him about Adrienne's psychotic episode at his place of business.

"I told you, bro. I'm done with that. Linda and I are going strong."

"That's want I want to hear. I'm glad to know you two are working things out."

Daron endured the rest of the grueling lecture from his older brother about love, marriage, and commitment. By the end of the conversation, he felt ashamed of how he carried on with

Adrienne and promised himself to be a better husband. He even hoped to convince his wife to start a family soon. As for Adrienne, he was sure she had already moved on. He hadn't heard any more from her. He assumed that whatever feelings she had for him had dissipated.

She's young. I'm sure she's in love with some young stud by now.

"So, how long will you be in town for?" Daron asked as the two stood up after paying for their drinks.

Daron could tell Derek was still bothered after hearing more details about the affair. He hoped he'd said enough to convince his brother that he was seriously working on saving his marriage. Having his brother be proud of him was important to Daron.

"I have some things to take care of early in the morning. Then I'll head back. Brianna's play is tomorrow night. I can't miss it."

The brothers walked outside and spoke for a few minutes more.

"Take care of Linda, dude. These young girls ain't no good for you."

Daron silently nodded as he watched Derek disappear down the street, feeling ashamed that his older brother knew the truth about his disgraceful indiscretions. He jumped into his truck and sat there for a few minutes. As the truck idled, Daron thought he smelled a faint scent of perfume. It reminded him of Adrienne. Whatever it was, it brought back familiar memories of the episodes that took place in his backseat. For a moment, the faint scent aroused him. He glanced at the seat behind him and reminisced about the sexual encounters. *No.*

He started the ignition and turned up the music. He needed something to distract him from the thoughts of temptation. Before pulling off, he looked in his rearview mirror. It was dark, he saw a familiar face standing at the corner of the street behind him from his mirror. *What the—?*

His heart pounded faster than ever. Daron rolled down his window and stuck out his head to get a better view. Whoever he thought he saw in the rearview mirror was now gone into the night. Believing it was all just his imagination, he sped off and headed home to his wife.

Chapter Twenty-Five
Desperate Transformation

She knew she had a problem but was afraid to admit it to herself openly. Adrienne was officially a stalker, and while she knew what she was doing was wrong, she justified her actions by telling herself it was all in preparation for her future life with Daron.

He will leave Linda one of these days, and I will be right there to take her place.

She was so absorbed with the couple's lives that it began to change her—her habits, her mannerisms, even the way she spoke. Staci and Jacki noticed the changes with Adrienne and often found her difficult to deal with.

"What's going on with you?" Jacki asked one day. "Hey, girl, I'm liking your new transformation and all—dressing up all the time, going to all these high-class places. But you're starting to act snooty and stuff. You even talk different."

While Adrienne desperately wanted to transform into the woman she believed Daron would fall in love with, she didn't like how the girls called her out about her self-improvement. She quickly dismissed them as simply jealous and considered finding new friends while she scrolled through Linda's list of friends on her social media page.

*****

Does he ever miss me? Adrienne wondered about Daron as she watched him leaving his sports club one evening. She still watched the couple frequently, only to end up returning home feeling sad and empty and spending the rest of the evening sulking alone in her bedroom.

The day after Thanksgiving, Linda posted a picture of herself sitting outside enjoying the sun at their home in the Keys. When Adrienne saw it, it gave her a sense of relief.

Good! She's gone for the winter.

Trying to keep up with Linda was exhausting. Now she could concentrate more on what Daron was doing—at least until he followed Linda to the Keys in another couple of weeks.

In two weeks, that is exactly what happened. Adrienne noticed the empty parking space in the lot when she passed by his company. Then several nights in a row, she drove by their house and found all the lights off each time. With the assurance that the couple was out of town, she considered spending more time with her own family. It had been a long time since she had done so.

*****

Many of Adrienne's co-workers knew about Daron because she always talked about him and referred to him as the man she was dating. As far as they knew, she spent a lot of time with him at his home in Scarsdale and even showed them pictures of herself by the pool. Her imaginary relationship boosted her confidence around the office, and she walked around the office proudly, knowing everyone was aware of the handsome, successful businessman who'd come and swept her off her feet.

"Well, is he coming to the Christmas party?" asked Marta, one of Adrienne's co-workers.

"I'm not sure. He's very busy with his business this time of year. But I'll try to convince him to stop by so everyone can meet him."

Adrienne knew she was setting herself up again, but telling the truth about him spending time in the Keys with his wife wouldn't have been too impressive. She couldn't resist being the center of attention when she shared the adventures that she and Daron did each weekend. The truth is she was sharing the activities he and Linda did as she watched from a distance.

"He may not come to the party, but he's taking me to Neiman's this weekend to shop for a dress. I have my eye on this cute Dolce and Gabbana," Adrienne added as she envisioned the racks of dresses in Linda's closet.

Since discovering Linda's high-end wardrobe, Adrienne kept abreast with the designer labels in the couture section at Neiman's. She had to make sure she spoke from experience.

"Oh, how nice. It seems like you have a great guy. My husband has no patience when it comes to shopping with me," Marta shared.

"Well, Daron loves to do it because he knows it makes me happy."

Deep inside, she knew she was taking it too far with her story about shopping for the dress. It reminded her of the previous year when she scrambled around looking for a dress to wear to Staci's New Year's Eve party. Adrienne ended up helping herself to whatever she wanted from Linda's closet. Just thinking about it again aroused her temptation. *After all, they're both out of town.* There was plenty of room for opportunity. She played it out in her mind, then quickly dismissed the idea. It had been a while since pulling off something like that. *No, it's crazy.*

By lunchtime, two other co-workers, Ginger and Monique,

approached Adrienne in the breakroom.

"So, I hear this rich, fancy man of yours is buying your dress from Neiman's," Ginger teased.

The two women laughed, but Adrienne didn't laugh with them. The fact that they mentioned Daron only indicated people were gossiping about her. She couldn't blame them. Adrienne had been stringing everyone along when it came to Daron. After all the talk about him, no one had seen him yet. But what could she do about it now? She was beginning to think she'd gotten herself in way too deep.

"As I said before, yes. He *appreciates* me. Therefore, he has no problem buying me what I *want*. Anything *else*?"

Adrienne's indignant tone was her way of letting the women know she was not tolerating being the office gossip. Looking embarrassed, Ginger took one step back, and Monique followed suit.

"Sorry, I was just curious," Ginger responded softly as she backed out of the breakroom.

Adrienne glared at the two of them until they disappeared into the hallway. She hoped it meant the end of the discussion about the dress. She was growing tired of keeping up this façade and started to regret ever mentioning him. It wasn't just the pressure of having an imaginary boyfriend. The thought of showing up in a new dress gave her anxiety.

*****

That evening, Adrienne shopped all over town for a dress suitable enough to look like something from haute couture. She wasn't even sure if she wanted to go to the upcoming Christmas party, especially alone.

Adrienne sighed and dragged her feet as she walked from shop to shop. The more she browsed, the more frustrated she became. Every dress she tried on either cost too much or didn't fit her the way she wanted and would need to be altered. With the Christmas party only a day away, she was running out of time. If only she could find the perfect dress, she would make a brief appearance at the party, make up an excuse for having to leave, and then return the dress the next day. After spending her time looking until closing, Adrienne left the mall empty-handed and mentally drained. Once she arrived home, she headed straight to bed. Adrienne needed to think things through.

*****

It was Friday morning, the day of the party. Adrienne spent the night tossing and turning, and by now, she had already worked out the details of her plan. She headed to the kitchen, where her mother was finishing her coffee before heading out to work.

"Would you like some pancakes?" her mother asked as she motioned towards the stack left on the counter.

"Sure, why not?" Adrienne answered.

She reached for a plate in the cabinet, but her mother quickly intervened.

"Let me do that. I'll make the plate for you."

"Thanks, Mom."

Adrienne poured herself a glass of orange juice and took a seat at the other end of the table. Her mother fixed Adrienne's plate of pancakes and turkey bacon, then handed her daughter the syrup as she sat down with her own plate.

"We never have breakfast together anymore," Adrienne said.

"Remember when I used to make cinnamon French toast with bananas for you and your sister on Saturday mornings, and we would all watch cartoons together?"

"Yes, Mom, I remember," Adrienne replied.

A wave of guilt overcame her as she realized how distant she had been from her mother and sister over the past year. She was so engrossed with Daron and Linda that she stopped paying attention to the family that had been nothing less than supportive of her. Adrienne looked at her mother and noticed the crow's feet around her eyes and the strands of gray that emerged from her once vibrant brown hair, realizing how she had aged over the past year. Adrienne knew how much her mother worried about her. She often hinted to Adrienne about her concerns.

"Adrienne, I just don't want things to end up like before," she once said.

Her mother had every reason to feel that way. If things weren't happening like before, they were heading in that direction now. However, she assured her mother she was not that same person.

"I'm okay, Mom. I'm just having fun with friends."

Her mother sipped on her coffee while watching Adrienne enjoy her breakfast. She often wondered what was going on with her daughter. She noticed the changes—the mood swings, the impulsive acts of running out the house to go God knows where in the middle of the night, the way she locked herself in her room for hours without speaking to anyone. In addition, she wondered how Adrienne was getting all the expensive clothes? *I saw those pictures of her in that Burberry bikini on Facebook.* She just prayed it wasn't coming to what happened before; she couldn't bear to go through that again.

"Well, I'm going to get ready for work," her mother told her.

She placed her coffee mug in the sink and kissed Adrienne lightly on the cheek. Adrienne smiled as she chewed her mouthful of food.

"Thanks for breakfast, Mom,"

Adrienne felt bad about not spending time with her mother and sister. In fact, she didn't know much about her younger sister's life. She overheard bits and pieces of their conversations about the good grades Kara was getting in school and how she tried out for the cheerleading squad. Adrienne assumed she made the team because she remembered once seeing some type of uniform hanging up in the laundry room. Adrienne never even saw Kara in her winter formal dress.

She promised herself that she would start paying more attention to her family. Her mother had always been there for her, and Kara could have used a big sister this past year.

Tomorrow.

Adrienne nodded to herself. Tomorrow she would wake up and cook them breakfast, and they would all spend the day together. She might even call her dad—something she had been avoiding as much as she could since the incident.

Tomorrow will be the start of building a better relationship with my family.

Chapter Twenty-Six

Poinsettias Everywhere

After her mother and Kara left for the day, Adrienne dressed in a pair of sweats, a black hoodie, sneakers, and a baseball cap before heading out the door. With the spare set of keys safely tucked in her pocket, she drove to Scarsdale, where she swung into her usual parking space at the church lot.

Although it was a frigid day, the sun gleamed brighter than it had all week. Adrienne looked up and let the warmth of the sunbeam on her face. She couldn't wait until the hot weather returned and already had plans up her sleeve for the upcoming summer.

She quickly walked down the tree-lined road and turned into the densely wooded lot. Halfway through, an uncomfortable feeling in her stomach caused her to stop in her tracks. For a second, she contemplated turning around and heading back.

I can just tell everyone I'm sick and not go to the party.

She stood there, in the middle of the brush, considering alternative plans instead of what she was about to do. *Is this dress really that important?* Adrienne slowly walked a couple of steps further, still weighing her options until the red tiles of the roof appeared in the distance. She was so close now; she could get it over with and be back through the woods in no time.

The sound of twigs snapping underneath her feet echoed into the air and startled Adrienne. She reminded herself there was no need to worry. *No one is home. Keep going.*

She hopped over the wall when she reached the backyard's perimeter and calmly walked across the lawn to the side door. As she unlocked the door, she recalled Daron's threat if she dared to contact Linda and the scorned look on his face at the anniversary dinner. It was finally becoming clear to her that perhaps she should move on with her life.

Just let them be, a voice told her.

At that moment, she promised herself it would be the last time she would enter the couple's home. In the meantime, she had her heart set on the dress and couldn't wait to slip it on. She had already convinced herself that her co-workers were expecting to see her in it, too, and she had to look stunning for them.

I'll be in and out of here in no time.

Once inside, she took off her sneakers, then walked through the laundry room and into the central part of the house. There was an unusual feel about the house, but Adrienne couldn't pinpoint what it was as she was too fixated on the dress. As she hurried through the long hallway, a whiff of pine tingled her nose, reminding her Christmas was just around the corner. She immediately thought of the awful experience she had with Daron last Christmas but quickly dismissed it. She was focused on looking fabulous tonight.

Adrienne bypassed the living room, family room, and Linda's office and made a beeline down the hall until she reached the staircase leading to the upstairs bedroom. At the bottom of the steps, the grandfather clock that stood against the wall appeared to tick louder than usual. She glanced at the time.

11:35 a.m. I'm sure they're basking in the sun and enjoying brunch at the pool by now.

As she headed up the stairs, she rolled her eyes at the thought of the couple sipping on mimosas. Once inside the master bedroom, she marched straight to Linda's closet to look for *her* dress. She couldn't wait to put it on. When she spotted the red one, Adrienne pulled it off its hanger and held it up in front of her. The beautiful Dolce & Gabbana that Linda wore for their anniversary dinner was the perfect dress for the night.

She quickly pulled off her clothes and slid into the luxurious, red satin material. The dress fit perfectly, and it transformed her small frame into the body of a sexy mature woman.

Damn, I'm fine.

Spinning around several times while looking in the tri-fold mirror, Adrienne couldn't help but smile as she appreciated how the dress effortlessly hugged her curves. She ran her fingers through her hair, pulled it up into a twist, and grabbed a rhinestone hair clip from the top of the jewelry armoire. Then she selected a pair of silver and rhinestone strapped heels and slipped her foot in one. The heel height was just right, so she picked up the other and placed them in a small duffle bag she brought along.

She turned to leave when suddenly the sound of a slamming door echoed from somewhere downstairs. Her heart pounded rapidly as she stood frozen—too afraid to move. She prayed she was only imagining the sounds of footsteps coming up the stairs.

Who'd be here now?

Adrienne's first reaction was to hide under the bed, but in a panic, she threw on her sweats, pulled the hooded sweatshirt over the dress, and ran out into the hallway. Linda was just as startled to see Adrienne as the two stood face-to-face at the top of the stairs. Linda was wearing jeans, tall riding boots, and a thick turtleneck sweater. Adrienne stood there speechless, unable to move, yet still managed to take note of Linda's casual attire; she had never seen her in jeans before. In a quick second, Linda let out a loud, piercing shriek. Adrienne screamed, too, as she stood barefoot, still clad in the red dress that hung from underneath her sweatshirt.

"Who the hell are you?" Linda asked.

She sounded frightened yet angry as she stood in a T-stance with clenched fists at her sides, prepared to fight the young intruder standing in front of her.

Adrienne attempted to run past her, but Linda grabbed her by the arm, and the two engaged in a struggle. The tightness of Linda's grip surprised Adrienne, who pulled with full force to try to release herself from the stronghold. All the while, Adrienne could barely stand Linda's loud screaming that was piercing to her ears; something about *stealing, dress, police,* and *arrested* was all she could make out.

Why won't she shut up?

Finally, Adrienne managed to pull one arm out from Linda's grip. She tried to pry Linda's other hand away, but Linda's hold only tightened. In an effort to escape, she grabbed the closest thing available—the bronze statue from the pedestal at the top of the stairs—and hit Linda over her head. In an instant, the screaming stopped. Blood immediately gushed from Linda's scalp, trickling down her face and onto her beige sweater. Dazed and confused, Linda touched her forehead with her hand, and after seeing the blood on her fingertips, her facial expression went from confusion to shock. She reached for the banister, but her bloody hand couldn't get a good grip. Her feet slipped from underneath her, and she let out one last shrilling scream. Adrienne watched as Linda tumbled down the cold, hard tiled staircase and landed face down on the bottom step.

I just wanted the screaming to stop.

From the top of the stairs, Adrienne waited for Linda to move. While keeping her eyes on the lifeless figure, Adrienne pulled her arms out of the sweatshirt and slid the dress straps off her shoulders. She quickly pulled it down and stepped out of it, leaving the three-thousand-dollar garment crumpled on the floor. Slowly making her way down the stairs, Adrienne carefully stepped over the body. That was when she saw them. *Poinsettias everywhere.* At the bottom of the steps, on a pedestal next to the grandfather clock, on the long table in the hall.

She was in too much of a panic to comprehend; however, as she tiptoed past the entertainment room, colorful glowing lights hit the corner of her eye. She looked inside to find the seven-foot Christmas tree standing tall, decorated with giant red and gold ornaments and lights blinking in a colorful pattern. Still unable to comprehend what she was seeing, her eyes slowly moved down to the bottom of the tree, where an assortment of colorfully wrapped boxes in various shapes and sizes were stacked underneath. It wasn't until then that she realized the couple was spending their Christmas in New York. She had become too comfortable. She had become careless, and now she was caught. Fearing Daron would probably be on his way home, too, Adrienne ran to put on her sneakers and bolted out the side door.

It seemed as if the church parking lot was miles away. Adrienne ran as fast as she could across the backyard and into the thick, dense brush. The tears in her eyes blurred her vision, making it difficult to see where she was stepping. Suddenly, she tripped over a branch and fell face-first onto the cold, muddy ground. She cried even harder as she grabbed onto a low-hanging branch to pull herself up, wiping the mud from her hands onto her sweatpants. Once she made it to the road, Adrienne sprinted until she reached the lot and jumped into her car.

Adrienne pulled off immediately, driving recklessly through the streets of Scarsdale. There was a tight knot in her stomach, and she began to feel lightheaded. *Not now,* she thought as the nausea persisted to a point where she could no longer hold back. She swerved into a Starbucks parking lot and pulled into a space far away from the other cars. It was just in the nick of time that she swung open the car door and vomited onto the pavement. She wiped her mouth with the sleeve of her sweatshirt, then held her head down while grasping the steering wheel and trying to catch her breath. There, she cried for the next ten minutes.

I killed someone. I'm gonna be all over the news.

She imagined the media portraying her as the evil scorned lover in the headlines: *Twisted Lover's Dangerous Obsession Ends in Murder. News at Eleven.*

The nausea returned, and she leaned her head outside the driver's side door, releasing whatever else was left inside of her. She glanced at her face in the rearview mirror. Swollen and red, she hated who she saw. She began to feel the shame and embarrassment as she envisioned her mugshot plastered all over the television screens.

After finally gaining her composure, Adrienne started the ignition and pulled off. She drove with extreme caution to avoid any attention from the police. She just wanted to spend some time at home before being picked up and arrested for murder.

It was shortly before 1:00 p.m. when Adrienne arrived home. She took a shower, changed her clothes, and tossed the sweats on the floor of her closet. Sitting on the edge of her bed, she began thinking about what had just occurred, then turned on the TV to see if there were any reports of a murder in Scarsdale. After not finding anything on the news, she decided to start acting on the promise she made to herself earlier that morning. She would make the best of her time with her mother and Kara—at least for as long as she could.

Adrienne put in a load of laundry and then went to the kitchen to prepare dinner. For the first time in years, Adrienne was cooking dinner for her mother and Kara.

It'll be a nice surprise for them.

She nervously prepared the lemon chicken, macaroni and

cheese, and broccoli, and while everything was cooking, she started on the red velvet cake with cream cheese frosting.

By the time her mother and Kara came home, Adrienne had folded and put away all the laundry and had dinner waiting on the table. Her mother was so surprised that she looked like she was about to cry.

"What's the occasion?" she asked.

"I just wanted to do something nice for you," Adrienne told her.

Still shaken up from the day's events, Adrienne tried to disguise the quiver in her voice.

"Everything looks so lovely. Thank you, sweetie," her mother said as she kissed Adrienne on the cheek and squeezed her tightly. She had no idea this would be their last meal together for a very long time.

After dinner, Adrienne placed the dirty dishes in the dishwasher and cleaned up the kitchen while her mother and Kara sat in the living room enjoying their cake. She joined them shortly after cleaning up, and the three of them watched a couple of programs that their mother usually watched alone. It was an enjoyable evening, and Adrienne realized how good it felt to be with her family.

Around nine that evening, she remembered the Christmas party. After the day's ordeal, she had no intentions of showing up at the party. She no longer cared about impressing her co-workers. She did, however, want to let Marta know she wouldn't be there.

Adrienne went to her room to get her cellphone to text Marta, saying she wouldn't be making the party. She knew everyone was expecting to see her in the extravagant dress she had talked so much about.

Sorry, not feeling well. Must have been something I ate. Have a great time.

As soon as she sent the message, she immediately received a text back. It was a picture of Marta and a few other employees on the dancefloor having a great time. They all looked like they had been drinking a lot already, and Adrienne chuckled, knowing there would be much talk about it on Monday morning.

Adrienne was replying to the text message when she heard the doorbell ring. Kara must have answered the door because Adrienne heard her worried tone calling out to her mother.

"Mom! The police are here."

*****

Adrienne saw the hurtful look on her mother's face as the police officers escorted her out with her hands cuffed behind her back. Kara held on to her mother as they both wiped tears from their eyes.

"What's going on? What's going on?" Kara repeatedly asked while another officer stood before her mother writing notes on a pad.

Her mother looked baffled as she responded to the officer's questions and shook her head often. A female police officer placed Adrienne in the back of the police car while Kara and her mother watched from the door. It was the most hurtful experience they ever had to endure.

Adrienne suddenly felt like she were in the middle of a very long bad dream. She wondered if she had really done all those things she was being accused of. She remembered the police officer mentioning something about an assault, breaking and entering, and other charges she didn't quite understand. The only good thing about the situation is that she overheard Linda being questioned at the hospital.

She's still alive! Adrienne was relieved to hear the news. She may have wanted her out of the picture, but she never had any intentions of committing murder.

*****

Daron rushed to the hospital as soon as he heard about his wife being a victim of a home invasion. He blamed himself; it was his idea for the two of them to come back to New York for the Christmas holiday instead of spending it down in the Keys. They appreciated the warm sunny weather in Florida, but he missed having the white Christmases, too, and convinced Linda to change their plans for the holidays. They had only been back in New York for a few days. Daron handled business at the agency, while Linda spent her days shopping for gifts for friends and family.

How could this have happened in our neighborhood?

He arrived at the Emergency Room, where he found his wife very bruised and bandaged. He was told she was lucky to be alive after being hit over the head and pushed down the stairs. A detective, who had just finished taking notes, asked to speak with Daron outside. He agreed but wanted to see his wife first. She was somewhat incoherent and tried to recall the incident as her medication began to work in her system.

From what Daron understood, Linda had been out shopping but decided to come back to the house for a minute. Something about picking up a red dress to take to the dry cleaners. When Linda walked into the house, she saw a girl standing at the top of the steps wearing the same red dress. The girl attacked her, hitting Linda in the head with something, and then pushed her down the stairs.

What the hell? Daron was enraged. *Some young punk broke into our home and tried to steal Linda's clothes?*

It didn't make sense to him. Maybe Linda was so traumatized that she was getting confused.

Who would try on clothes in the middle of a robbery?

"Young. Pretty girl. Fan," Linda moaned as she tried to describe the perpetrator.

She closed her eyes and appeared to be in a lot of pain. Daron stood by her side, tightly clasping her hand as she struggled to speak. Tears rolled down her cheeks as she tried to explain something about some fan of hers who had broken into their house. Daron didn't realize Linda's popularity would cause a stir-crazed fan to act like this. He vowed to see that whoever did this would be fully prosecuted.

The police were on their job, canvassing the area and going door-to-door looking for any witnesses. Living in such an affluent neighborhood, not too much got past anyone, and anything suspicious was noted. There were only two houses on the private road where Daron and Linda lived. Daron's neighbors, Tom and wife Myrna, lived across the street. However, they were away in Europe for the holidays. On the main street, before turning onto the private road, one neighbor said they saw a young, pretty woman sprinting down the street. She was wearing sweats, and although the witness didn't recognize her, they thought she was a jogger from the neighborhood. Searching further, the police interviewed a couple of groundskeepers of the church at the end of the main street. They described a burgundy Kia parked in the back of the lot sometime during the morning. Both men assumed it belonged to one of the members of the congregation. Only one of them could remember part of the license plate's number because it was the same as his daughter's birthdate: 0522.

Fortunately, a newly installed security camera recorded the license plate of the car entering and leaving the church parking lot. The police ran a check on the plates, which revealed the car's registered owner. Meanwhile, Detective Watkins spoke with Daron and summarized what they knew so far: a witness stated seeing a young girl running down the street shortly after the incident. Other witnesses saw a car parked in the back of the church parking lot.

"Do you know of anyone who fits that description with that type of car?" the detective had asked.

"No," Daron lied. "I have no idea who that could be."

Daron felt a knot in his stomach; he immediately recognized

the car's description. The image of Adrienne running down the street entered his head. *She's been out of my life for months now.* He nervously jingled the change in his pocket as the detective continued his questioning. The fact that Adrienne was a possible suspect distracted him, and he heard very little the detective had to say. Once the detective finished, he excused himself to take a call.

Daron began to sweat, sensing his world was about to crash down on him. *What if they connect me to Adrienne? What would Linda say? What if she leaves me this time? Relax. It's probably not her.*

Later that evening, the detective returned to Daron with an update. The police had picked up the girl who owned the car. Detective Watkins gave him her name, and Daron took a minute to absorb the blow. His mouth went dry, and he swallowed hard before speaking. Then with every effort to hide his emotions, he denied knowing anyone named Adrienne Madison.

Chapter Twenty-Seven

Serial Stalker

After spending the weekend at the local holding facility, Adrienne was transported to the county jail, where she would stay until her trial. Everyone was devastated by the news of Adrienne's arrest. Thankfully, her father came through with a great attorney. Adrienne was grateful for him yet ashamed she would have to face her father at one of her lowest points...again.

Adrienne's attorney, Brett Mason, was a tall, gray-haired man who wore tailored suits and bright-colored ties. Adrienne thought he was handsome for an older man and particularly liked his style, even though his GQ fashion instantly reminded her of Daron. When she first met with him, he opened a folder with several documents inside and tried to explain the charges against her. Most of what he said was too technical for Adrienne to comprehend. Her head was already spinning from the ordeal of being in jail and lack of sleep. All she could understand was that she was in serious trouble and probably going to face some time. The severity of what she had done was beginning to set in, and it frightened her. She just wanted to go home.

Len Richelle

"So, what about bail?"

"They found your passport and some information indicating a search for a one-way ticket to Paris. Were you planning to kill this woman and then leave the country?"

"What? No, I was going on vacation. I–I was trying to figure out the cheapest—"

"Not a good look. A round-trip ticket would've looked less suspicious. That's what most people do. Who books a one-way trip to France?"

Brett looked at her and waited for an explanation. Reluctantly, she told him the embarrassing details.

"I had just received my passport and wanted to see Paris. I couldn't afford the price for a round-trip ticket, so I took a chance and bought the one-way ticket, hoping I would find a cheap flight back in a couple of days."

There was a moment of silence while Brett looked down at the paperwork and shook his head. Adrienne thought about the trip to Paris that Daron and Linda had taken for their anniversary. She had been obsessed with Paris ever since. She planned to take a trip, hopefully sometime after Christmas, and share her adventures with her co-workers. She was going to say Daron took her. Adrienne would feel like a fool having to explain that to him.

Brett studied the paperwork for a moment.

"Then you've got this prior charge," he continued. "What is this? Stalking? Assault? Trespassing? Sounds like the same kind of case. And you're still on probation for the previous case."

Brett sounded frustrated as he tossed the paperwork down on the table. He wanted to help Adrienne, but she looked like a serial stalker to him.

Adrienne held down her head. The nightmare was getting worse by the minute. She looked up to find Brett leaning in closer, and he spoke in a low voice as if to avoid anyone else from hearing.

"Adrienne, did you do this before? To someone else?"

Adrienne felt a hard lump in her throat, and although she tried to speak, the words could not come out. Finally, a tiny voice inside her began to whisper. ·

"Yes. He was a neighbor who used to live down the street."

*****

Explaining everything to Brett was like reliving it all over again. After spending the next hour listening to Adrienne tell her story, Brett stared at her in disbelief.

"It happened a few years ago, right before I graduated from high school." Adrienne twisted a piece of tissue in her hand as she recalled her shameful past. "I used to babysit for his little girl, Ariana. The mom worked a lot out of town, so I dealt with him most of the time. I could tell he liked me. He just wasn't ready to leave his wife, I guess. One day, she asked to meet me at the house. When I got there, the two of them were there together. She told me they no longer needed me. Something about me misunderstanding or something. Things got out of hand after that."

Adrienne stared at the wall away from Brett. He stared at Adrienne, waiting to hear the rest. She couldn't bear to relive the story. She had already paid her debt. *Why can't he just leave this alone?*

"Okay, Adrienne, what happened?"

"Nothing, really. They accused me of following them around."

"You mean *stalking*?"

"I didn't see it like that. I just wanted to know what he saw in her."

Tears rolled down Adrienne's cheek as she began to realize she had a problem. She thought this was all behind her, but she realized she was doing the same thing she had done in her past.

It was obvious Brett already knew the story; he just wanted to hear it from Adrienne. He stared at her and waited for her to continue.

"After they confronted me, I left the house upset. I had just gotten my license, so I ran back home and took my mother's car keys to go for a drive. I took off down the street and saw his wife pulling out of the driveway, so I followed her. She didn't know I was behind her. It was dark, so I know she couldn't tell it was me who bumped her and caused her to slide down into the ditch."

After what seemed like a long silence, Brett cleared his throat and adjusted his tie. Because of her age and no criminal history, Adrienne was let off easy and only had to do community service and probation, which she had now violated.

No one ever let Adrienne forget what she did. Her mother watched her like a hawk and questioned her whenever she thought she displayed unusual behavior, such as leaving home in the middle of the night or buying an expensive tennis outfit and racquet even though she had never played tennis. The same patterns Adrienne had before were very similar to her actions lately. With suspicions raised, her mother told Adrienne's father. When he tried to talk to Adrienne, she avoided him. Staci and Jacki noticed the signs, too, and Adrienne often caught them exchanging glances and raising eyebrows at some of her behavior. She pretended not to notice, but she knew they suspected she was setting herself up for something bad. They just didn't know what. The previous incident was why it was so hard to get close to her father again. He was the one who bailed her out of jail when she was arrested. The look in his eyes when he picked her up, knowing his daughter was a stalker who allegedly nearly mowed down her neighbor's wife... Well, Adrienne was so ashamed, she couldn't face him. Unfortunately, she had fallen again.

"I'll try to work with the judge on setting bail, but I can't guarantee you on this one," Brett said as he began putting the paperwork in his folder.

They talked more about the case. He was going back to court. Blah, blah, blah. Adrienne was in a daze. She heard nothing else as she tried to think of what could save herself from staying in there.

She didn't remember pushing Linda down the stairs. From her recollection, they were scuffling, and Linda slipped. However, according to Linda's statement, Adrienne hit her over the head with an object and then pushed her. Adrienne tried to remember the details of that day so she could defend herself. She would never intentionally hurt someone, let alone try to kill them. Then again, it was still all a blur to her.

Maybe I really am a hardened criminal.

Frightened by the possible outcome of the case, she held her head down and fought back the tears as the correctional officer escorted her down the long corridor to her cell.

*****

Her first visit with her mother was heartbreaking. When Adrienne walked into the visiting room, she spotted her mother right away, sitting at a table looking lost and distraught. With her hands clasped in front of her, she stared at a wall as if lost in space. Adrienne walked up to the table, and her mother gave her a tight squeeze. The two sat at the table, and Adrienne immediately noticed the red in her eyes as they swelled up with tears.

It was an extremely difficult visit. Adrienne thought about the promises she made to herself just hours before her arrest about spending more time with her mother and sister and appreciating her family more than she did. Now she realized she had lost the chance, at least for a very long time.

Her mother was emotional during the entire visit. She didn't understand how things had once again gotten out of control, and Adrienne was too ashamed to explain them to her. She looked in Adrienne's eyes for answers as to why her oldest daughter was still doing these things she promised she would never again do.

"Sweetheart, what's gotten into you? How can I help?" her mother asked.

She held Adrienne's hand tightly from across the table until the C.O. walked by and looked down at the two as if to give them a warning. She gently pulled away, placed her hands on her lap, and stared down at them.

"I can't explain, Mom. I just can't. But I want you to know I'm sorry for everything."

Her mother continued to sob and wiped away her tears with her sleeve.

"Please get you some help while you're in here, Adrienne," she said in a low voice.

Deep down, Adrienne knew her mother knew the real story. She knew how easily attached her daughter became to people. Not just people—men. Her mother didn't believe for one minute that this was all about Adrienne wanting to meet this author who everyone around town ranted and raved about.

"This was about him, wasn't it?" her mother asked.

During the time Adrienne had been seeing Daron, she never talked about him to her mother. However, her mother could see through Adrienne's behavior that some man had not only captured Adrienne's heart but broke it, too.

"You should call your father. He's worried about you."

"Dad?" said Adrienne.

She wasn't ready to face her father. What would he think of her now? What did Abby think of her stepdaughter? Adrienne felt nothing less than foolish and ashamed. The last thing she needed to know was that her father looked at her as a criminal.

After the visit, Adrienne informed her mother that there was no need to visit her while she was in the county jail. Perhaps she would welcome a visit once she transferred to her assigned prison, wherever that would be. For now, she was too ashamed to deal with anyone showing up to see her like she was a caged animal. Her mother looked heartbroken after hearing Adrienne's request, and the reality that her daughter would most likely be doing time started the tears to run down her cheek again until the C.O. passed by the table, indicating visiting hours were over.

Her mother gave Adrienne another tight squeeze, and Adrienne kissed her on the cheek. She thanked her mother for all her support and for hiring her attorney, then asked her to thank her father, as well.

"Think about writing or calling him. He loves you, no matter what," her mother said as she wiped away her tears.

"Maybe," she responded.

Adrienne watched as her mother walked out the visiting room door, then waited for the female officer to take her to the strip room. It was routine for an inmate to be strip-searched after a visit. It was another reason she wanted to cut back on the visits. Each experience was more humiliating than the next.

*****

Adrienne reached out to Jacki and Staci only a couple of times while in jail. It was only because they kept writing her insisting that she called. *Do you need money to call? Please call me or Jacki collect,* Adrienne had read in one of the many letters Staci wrote. Adrienne was ashamed of what she had done but knew she had to face her two best friends at some point.

She called Jacki first because she knew Jacki would be more understanding about her arrest. There were plenty of men Jacki dated who spent some time in one correctional facility or another. Jacki was used to taking the long drive upstate to one of the desolate towns where the prisons were located just to see any one of them. Adrienne was there for Jacki plenty of times when she vented about one of her men who unexpectedly got hauled away in a police car.

Yes, she would understand.

"I can't explain it over the phone," said Adrienne.

She was nervous about speaking to her friend, but Jacki was very casual, like all of this was something she was used to.

"I know how it is. When Jay was in jail, he couldn't say a lot over the phone either. Just be strong, girl. You'll be home soon. We'll all be here for you."

After her encouraging talk with Jacki, she reluctantly called Staci. The more judgmental of the two, Staci would most likely lecture her about morals and values. However, to Adrienne's surprise, Staci reacted better than expected.

"Do you need anything?" asked Staci. "I'll send you more money in the morning," she added the first time Adrienne called.

Her soft tone let Adrienne know she was not there to judge but only to be there for a longtime friend.

"No, but thanks. I just really appreciate your support," said Adrienne.

She tried to hold back the tears as Staci promised to look after her mother and Kara. Before the call ended, she assured Adrienne that everything would work out fine.

It was good to know her two closest friends were still there for her. They didn't pry, and Adrienne never had to explain the whole truth about what she had done.

*****

"Here's the deal. You plead guilty to Trespassing and Simple Assault. That's a huge step down from the charges you should be facing. You're an impressionable young lady, and you admired her as a creative writer. You've read all her books. Blah, blah, blah. Followed all her social media, watched her every move. Fell in love with her, if you will, and found out where she lived. Admit you took a chance, walked into an unlocked door, and tried on a couple of dresses. She came home; you panicked and tried to run. You never meant to hurt her. Judge gives you a year or less. However, you're still on probation from the last incident. So, most likely, you'll get some time added to your sentence. Good behavior is you're saving grace to get out sooner. Okay?"

Brett looked frustrated yet satisfied with the plea he laid out before her.

It turns out Daron wanted this to go away just as bad as Adrienne. Somehow, he had the prosecutor negotiate a deal with Adrienne's attorney so certain pieces of information would never be disclosed. No one would know about the affair, and as much money Daron underhandedly paid both attorneys, no one ever will. Fortunately for Adrienne, no one—including Daron—found out about her stalking or the fact that she had broken into the home more than once. Linda was clueless and genuinely believed Adrienne was just a young, crazy fan. She never put together that Daron had anything to do with Adrienne.

Adrienne agreed to the plea and anxiously waited to appear in court.

On the day of sentencing, Linda was there dressed to the nines as usual, and right by her side, being the supportive husband, was Daron. Adrienne caught a glimpse of them sitting on the other side of the courtroom. With a serious facial expression, Daron looked straight ahead while Linda occasionally looked in Adrienne's direction. Adrienne felt the humiliation as she glanced at the perfect-looking couple across the room while she sat on the other side wearing a modest navy-blue dress that was two sizes too big. *It was all I could find that wasn't too revealing,* her mother had told her. Her mother did her best to select a suitable dress for Adrienne to wear for the sentencing, but the clothes in Adrienne's closet were not appropriate for court.

During the Victim Impact phase, Linda assured the judge that she felt no anger towards Adrienne and hoped Adrienne received all the treatment she needed to have a bright future.

"Your Honor, I would even like to mentor her someday."

Adrienne figured Daron must have done a good job convincing Linda that Adrienne was just a young lost girl who wanted to follow in Linda's footsteps.

Adrienne anxiously tapped her foot as she listened to Linda speak so eloquently about her. It was as if she was attending one of Linda's book launches, and Linda was standing in front of her fans reading excerpts from her latest novel. This time, the story was about a young girl who may have taken the wrong path but has a chance to be saved. Linda would be her hero.

My hero. Adrienne chuckled to herself as she listened to her ex-lover's wife ramble on about turning a misguided girl into someone with a purposeful life. Adrienne maintained a somber facial expression, but she could barely refrain from shouting out loud that she had done all of this because of her love for Daron. She tuned herself out from the sound of Linda's voice as she imagined how it would all play out.

I interrupt Linda right about now. I let her and everyone know I did this all for Daron. I'm in love with Daron. The entire court gasps; they're all in shock. There's a lot of chattering among the spectators. The judge bangs his gavel to quiet the crowd. Linda looks at me with rage in her eyes and yells, "No, he's my husband." Then Daron stands up and announces he loves me, too. The crowd gasps even louder, ignoring the judge's demands for order in his court.

"Just be grateful," whispered Brett.

Adrienne snapped out of her fantasy as Brett squeezed her shoulder and leaned in closely.

"He just wants you to leave them alone."

Brett was referring to Daron, whom she was now convinced had paid off several people to make this all go the way he wanted. Adrienne would accept it for what it was. After all, it could have been a lot worse. The only thing that baffled Adrienne was that both he and Linda were in New York during the winter.

I had just looked at pictures of them in front of palm trees.

Adrienne remembered the voice in her head that kept warning her about going into the house.

Maybe I should listen to myself sometimes.

The sound of the judge's gavel indicated the session was over. A female court officer came to Adrienne's side and cuffed her hands behind her back. She heard a few sniffles directly behind her, and as she turned to leave, she looked over her shoulder. There they were sitting on the benches behind her: her mother, Kara, Staci, Jacki, her father, and her stepmother, Abby.

Chapter Twenty-Eight

Yes, I'm Fully Rehabilitated

"So, are you excited about coming home?" asked Staci.

Staci and Jacki were visiting Adrienne, and the three sat in the outdoor visiting area. Adrienne had given them the news that she would be released earlier than expected. Her good behavior and programming allowed her the extra time off.

"Of course, I am. I can't wait to get out of this prison hole, and I can't wait to get back into nice clothes. These khakis aren't exactly designer," Adrienne said, chuckling at her effortless joke.

She noticed Staci and Jacki glancing at each other.

"What's up? What's going on?" asked Adrienne.

She looked at Jacki, who quickly looked away. Then she turned to Staci, who finally spoke up.

"We love you, Adrienne. You're like a little sister to us. We–we just wanted to make sure…"

Staci hesitated and looked at Jacki for assistance. Jacki bluntly took the lead.

"We want to make sure you're fully rehabilitated—that you

won't stalk anybody anymore."

There was a moment of silence, and Adrienne felt uncomfortable having to face her two friends and convince them that she could be normal. However, she knew it would take a while before anyone believed her again.

"Yes, I've changed," replied Adrienne confidently.

She understood why her friends would be skeptical and wanted to assure them that they didn't need to be. She sat up straight in her chair and looked them both in the eyes.

"I'm fully rehabilitated."

The two nodded at each other, and both women let out a sigh of relief. Adrienne was sure she had convinced her friends that things would be different. When she was released from prison, her actions would prove it. She was looking forward to having another chance.

After the first few months in prison, Adrienne's feelings for him began to fade. She even laughed at herself, realizing how silly it was to want to be like Linda. During her incarceration, she participated in several women's groups that taught her how to overcome her self-esteem, self-confidence, and impulse control issues. She learned she didn't need material things to impress other people. She was smart, attractive, and if she opened up more often, people would see the good qualities she possessed without her having to lie to impress anyone. She was ready to come home and show the world the new and improved Adrienne. She was prepared to start a new life, meet new people, and forget her past. She was ready.

For the next two months, she finished up a couple of classes, updated her résumé, and made plans for her release. Before she went home, she had one last session with the prison psychologist. Dr. Ray helped Adrienne through many of her issues, and it was time to thank her for all she had done.

"How do you feel?" Dr. Ray asked.

Adrienne sat comfortably in the chair, facing Dr. Ray. She studied Dr. Ray's face. Her auburn hair was beginning to reveal the gray roots, and her eyes had dark circles underneath them. Adrienne thought Dr. Ray must hear a lot of crazy stories such as hers. She wondered about all the other inmates who sat in the same chair. Were they as troubled as she had been? She looked around the room and realized she had made a lot of progress from being the timid young girl who arrived there nearly two years ago.

"I'm great! I'm excited to be going home," Adrienne replied.

Dr. Ray put down her pad and placed her clasped hands atop her desk. She smiled at Adrienne and nodded at her response.

"Yes, I heard you were getting out a little earlier with your good behavior. Well, that's good. Just remember the things we discussed here. And remember the exercises we went over. You are going to be just fine. You've come a long way."

Adrienne blushed and smiled back. She believed it, too, and thanked Dr. Ray for all of her help. That was the last time she spoke with the psychologist, and as she walked down the corridor towards her housing unit, she reminisced about the lessons learned in the last several years of her life. She summed them up as a means of growth and now considered herself a more confident, secure young woman who recognized her self-worth. She couldn't imagine herself falling for another Daron. She was just too good for settling to be someone's second best, let alone creeping with someone else's husband.

What was I thinking?

She entered her housing unit and walked into her cell. She had just gotten a new cellmate who was a couple of years younger than Adrienne. Trisha seemed just as timid and meek as Adrienne was when she first arrived. Since her arrival only a few days ago, she clung to Adrienne and looked to her for guidance when doing anything around the prison. Trisha reminded Adrienne of her younger sister, Kara. Although they had only been sharing a cell for a few days, Adrienne took on the responsibility to teach Trisha the ins and outs of prison life, and she even lectured her on life experiences, particularly about men.

"Don't settle, especially for someone else's man," Adrienne advised.

Trisha, who was a little confused at her statement, looked at Adrienne and shrugged her shoulders while Adrienne continued.

"Know your worth. You'll see. Making bad choices in men always leads to no good."

Trisha nodded, then went back to skimming through her magazine. She didn't particularly care for Adrienne's daily lectures, but she let Adrienne talk anyway. It was obvious Adrienne had been through something that must have taught her a big lesson.

Whatever she did, I'll make sure I won't do the same.

Chapter Twenty-Nine

A Fresh Start

Linda continued to write books and occasionally teach at the university. However, she often had trouble working out of her home office since the incident and especially if she was in the house alone. "The quiet in this house gives me the creeps," she had told Daron, who suggested she use her office at the university more often. So, she decided to drive there daily to be out of the house.

After several months, Linda finally began to feel comfortable talking about her ordeal. One night, she and Daron had gone out for dinner with friends. They met up with David and Deborah at one of Linda's favorite soul food restaurants. Everyone was enjoying themselves—laughing, joking, and catching up on each other's lives. Of course, the subject eventually came up.

"You don't have to talk about it if you don't want, but you know you can always count on me for support," said Deborah.

"I know, hun, and thank you. I'm doing well. We both are." Linda smiled at Daron and tightly squeezed his hand.

"So, what's up with that girl? Was she crazy or something?" asked David.

"You know, just a young fan of mine who was trying to get close. That's all." Linda scooped up a few grains of rice on her fork, then let them fall back onto her plate.

Daron took a gulp of his ice water. He dreaded having this conversation. To this day, Linda never knew the real story behind Adrienne, and it made him nervous knowing that she would eventually bring it up again. It also annoyed him how self-centered she was—believing the only reason Adrienne was after her was because she was an obsessed fan—and how Linda turned herself into the hero. However, if that were enough to keep Linda from prying further about Adrienne, he would learn to live with her recollection of the incident.

"So, did she get a lot of time?" Deborah asked.

Linda shook her head while chewing on a small piece of her roll.

"Not much. I asked the judge to be lenient."

"You what?" Deborah scoffed. "I would've put that girl *under* the jail if it was me."

"Some people might think like that," said Linda. "However, I know she's had some troubles. I'd like to mentor her someday."

Daron looked at Linda, nearly choking on the water he was sipping. He immediately called the waiter and asked for a vodka tonic.

"Babe," he said, turning to Linda, "do you think that's a good idea? I mean, she pushed you down the stairs."

"And I *forgave* her," said Linda. "Yes, she broke into my home, but she was a huge fan of mine. I mean, look at how many books I've written!"

Daron rolled his eyes. At that instant, he almost wanted her to know the truth. *Maybe that'll humble her.*

"There are too many young men and women already in the system. I believe wholeheartedly that most of them just need guidance and some attention. I couldn't bear to see that young girl ruined by the prison system. Besides, when I heard her in

236

court reading her letter of apology, my heart nearly melted. She could probably be as great a writer as me. I think she'd make a great storyteller."

As the rest of the evening went on, Daron ate his food in silence. He listened as Linda proudly told the story about the break-in—how Adrienne was caught trying to steal her couture dress—and even joked about Adrienne having good taste in clothing. Linda continued with her story of heroism as she fought with Adrienne until she was viciously pushed down the stairs.

"Luckily for her, if it wasn't for my fall, I don't know how much damage I would have done to that young girl."

Daron knew Linda would never change. She would always brag about something or another. He had already accepted it, although he didn't always agree with it.

I guess everyone has their flaws. Surely, I have mine.

After dinner, the couples said their goodbyes while waiting for the valets to bring their cars. On the ride home, Linda seemed in much better spirits than she had been in a long time. Daron glanced at her as he was driving and caught her smiling while gazing out the window.

"Hey, hun. What are you thinking?"

He grabbed her hand and squeezed it.

"Babe, I've wanted to tell you something for a while now."

Linda shifted herself in the seat to look at Daron, who slowed down the car as he looked over at her.

"What's going on?"

"I'm ready to have a baby. What about you?"

*****

By the time they pulled into the garage, Daron and Linda were discussing baby names. Daron Junior if it was a boy, and Lauren, Linda's pen name, if they had a girl. The two were so excited about their new plans that they began acting like the young and in-love couple they used to be and started stripping off their clothes while making their way to the bedroom. Daron was happy that they were going to focus on what he had desired for so long—a child to carry on his legacy. This would be the start of their family. A fresh start.

From that point on, they put their mistakes behind them and continued to focus on each other and their soon-to-be bundle of joy. Linda decided to put off publishing any new books, and the two concentrated on making a baby. It was a joyous time for them, and any trace of the negative past had practically disappeared for good. The worst was now behind them.

Chapter Thirty

Released...?

It was like one of those movie scenes when the tall barb-wired gate slowly opens and the prisoner, who hasn't seen the light of day in years, walks out to freedom. It was 9:30 a.m., and Adrienne's mother and sister were right on time, waiting for her at the rear gate. She walked quickly towards them and saw tears in her mother's eyes before she even got close to her.

"I'm so happy you're back with us," her mother said, wiping her tears while holding her daughter tightly.

Adrienne hugged her with all her might. She hadn't forgotten the promises she made before being arrested. As soon as she got in the car, Kara immediately began asking a slew of questions about her incarceration.

"Wait a minute, Kara," their mother interrupted. "Let Adrienne have a moment. We'll get something to eat, then go home and talk. That's if she wants to talk about it."

Her mother looked at Adrienne and squeezed her hand. Adrienne looked back at her and smiled. She thought about how much she appreciated her. Her mother was right. Adrienne needed to absorb that she was free and enjoy the breeze blowing through the window.

They stopped at a nearby restaurant to have lunch. It was the best meal she'd had in a couple of years, and she barely stopped to take a breath until she was done with the last bit of dessert.

Arriving home was surreal. Adrienne walked slowly through the front door and took the time to recall the familiar scent. It gave her a warm, comforting feeling that reminded her of everything good. Looking back, she hated herself for being so self-centered and never valuing the family she had. She spent many days in prison thinking about all the good things she would do for her family. Today was the day she would start.

Before joining her mother and Kara in the living room, Adrienne wanted to spend some time alone in her room. She had come home in the ugly, gray sweats she purchased while in prison, so she couldn't wait to change into nicer clothes that reminded her of being free.

She found a new colorful comforter covering her bed. There were new curtains on the windows, and the room was bright and freshly cleaned. Her mother had taken the time to make sure Adrienne's room was ready for her return. The first thing she did was go into her jewelry box and take out the heart pendant that her father had given her long ago. She put on the necklace and reminded herself that she would call him that evening. She would make plans to meet him for lunch the next day.

"Do you think you can still fit into your dress clothes for your job interviews?" her mother asked as she stood in the doorway.

"Good question. I'll look through the closet and see what fits."

"Okay, well, let me know. If you need something new to wear, we can go shopping this weekend."

She left Adrienne in the room to sort through her clothes.

"Thanks, Mom," Adrienne called out as her mother

disappeared down the hallway.

Adrienne opened the sliding door to her closet and pulled out a few of her work suits. Prison food was horrible, and with all the stress she had gone through, she seldom had much of an appetite. So, she was sure she had lost several pounds. She tried on a couple of skirts, and although they fit loosely, she could still wear them for job interviews.

Rummaging through her old clothes put Adrienne in a great mood. She couldn't wait to get back to working a real job. She began picking through the rack—pulling out various blazers, blouses, and pants—and trying them on in the mirror. Adrienne remembered purchasing some of the items when she first began working for Daron's company and how she bought only the clothes that enhanced her curvy figure so that he would notice.

How silly of me. Adrienne laughed it off and continued going through the rack. The sexy black dress she had worn on her first night with Daron was in the back of her closet. It was a bittersweet memory, but rather than dwell on the past, she placed it back on the rack and turned to her dresser drawers. Everything was still in its place, neatly folded and organized.

Adrienne decided to take a shower before relaxing with her mother and Kara, who were waiting for her in the living room. She couldn't wait to catch up on everything that had happened since she was gone and knew they were interested in hearing about her time while in prison.

After showering, Adrienne pulled out a pair of sweatpants and searched the closet for the matching sweatshirt. She usually kept them together and couldn't understand why they were not in the same place. After another thorough search, she found the sweatshirt hanging up on the other side of the closet. She assumed her mother had found the item on the floor when the police came to get her. Her mother would have been the only one to have placed it on a hanger.

"Adrienne!" yelled Kara. "I'm making popcorn! Want

some?"

"Sure, Kara! Be right there!"

As she pulled the sweatshirt over her head, she heard a slight jingle from the front pocket. She stood there for a moment, several thoughts racing in her head.

Two years in prison. No, no, no. It couldn't be.

Adrienne sat down on her bed, too afraid to acknowledge her feelings. The thought of it thrilled her, but she had worked so hard to move on. Finally, after several moments, Adrienne took a deep breath, reached into the pocket, and let her fingers trace the jagged edges of the items inside. For a second, she considered taking off the sweatshirt and throwing it in the trash. There were too many memories she was not fond of and spent the last two years trying to forget. She touched the items again, and a tingly feeling surged from the top of her head down to her toes. She needed to think responsibly, but the urges were strong.

No.

Maybe.

Adrienne smelled the popcorn from down the hall, and the buttery aroma snapped her out of the daze. She pulled out the set of keys with the handwritten tag labeled *HOME* and put them in her secret hiding spot.

As she walked out into the hallway, she shrugged her shoulders while thinking to herself, *Who knows what I'll do with them. Time will only tell.*

Epilogue

Amber Eyes

It was a rainy Thanksgiving evening, and Daron cautiously handled the slippery roads on the drive home. He and Linda had just spent the holiday having dinner with family. The night was even more special because it was the first time everyone got to see the new addition to the family.

"She has your eyes, Daron," his Aunt Ellie commented.

"Yes, but she has all of Linda's other beautiful features," he said proudly.

Relatives cooed in awe over baby Lauren Simone, now four months old, as she made her debut into the Weathers' clan.

"It looks like our daughter stole the show," said Linda.

She reached over into the car seat and gently touched baby Lauren's cheek with her fingertip. She admired her beautiful daughter as she slept quietly in the backseat.

Daron was in a hurry to get back to their Scarsdale home. He wanted to get his newborn daughter out of the cold, damp weather and spend a couple of hours with his wife by the fireplace.

He glanced into the rearview mirror to get a glimpse of his precious daughter. He and Linda had come a long way since the events from a few years ago. After Adrienne went to prison, he did everything to make the marriage work. To him, the break-in was like a near-death experience—meaning if Linda had found out who Adrienne really was, he would have just died. That is if Linda didn't kill him first. He paid a hefty fee to his lawyers to work things out so Linda would think Adrienne was nothing more than a fan of hers. For once, he was happy Linda's vanity had her believing it.

They were passing the church near their home when something caught Linda's attention.

"Who on Earth would be jogging in this weather?" she asked.

Daron looked at Linda as she pointed at the small image running past them. He looked in the rearview mirror to catch a glimpse of the petite figure wearing a dark hoodie and running down the street. He made the left turn onto the private road and turned up the long cobblestone driveway.

"Did you see?" asked Linda.

Daron could barely get the words out. He didn't want to believe what he saw. *No, it couldn't be.*

"N–no, I–I didn't see anyone."

In his mind, he knew who he saw, but he quickly dismissed his idea to paranoia.

"I could have sworn it was a young girl running in the rain. I guess I'm just tired."

Daron drove up the driveway in silence. Once inside the garage, he took a deep breath, then turned around to get another look at his beautiful baby. He wouldn't let anything come between him and his family anymore.

As they got out of the car, Linda grabbed the car seat and carried baby Lauren inside. Daron stood in the garage a moment longer. He took several deep breaths to calm his pounding heart. The image was still in his mind. He didn't see her face, but her petite, curvy silhouette said it all.

He walked into the house and locked the door behind him.

Linda was already upstairs, putting the baby to bed. Before heading up the stairs, Daron walked through the house, checking doors and windows and looking for anything out of place. He walked into the baby's room to find Linda sitting in the corner chair and gently rocking baby Lauren to sleep.

"I love you," he said, then blew a kiss to his wife.

Before walking towards their bedroom, Daron turned back.

"Oh, and babe," he said.

Linda looked up from admiring baby Lauren. "Yeah, babe?"

"Let's look into getting more security for the house tomorrow."

Linda stopped rocking and looked confused. Since the break-in, they already had another alarm system installed, and she had gotten into the practice of ensuring it was armed each time she left the house. What else did they need in this neighborhood?

"Sure. Whatever you say, babe," she replied, then continued rocking.

Daron went to his closet and began to undress. As he did, he noticed the neatly stacked sweaters and shirts on the shelves. Something seemed strange to him, but he couldn't figure out what. He shook his head and laughed at himself.

Boy, I'm paranoid, he thought, but the feeling was still there as he headed towards the shower.

*****

It didn't take long for baby Lauren to fall asleep. Linda carefully placed her in the crib, then leaned over to kiss her goodnight. She watched as her little girl took soft breaths while sleeping peacefully.

Linda thought of how fortunate she was to have a life full of so many blessings—her lovely home, her beautiful baby, her amazing career, her husband, and...*Derek.*

Linda and Daron's brother, Derek, had been secretly having

245

an affair for years. After Linda found out about one of Daron's affairs, she confided in Derek about leaving Daron. Linda was devastated and fed up. Derek was one of the few people she could openly vent about their marital issues.

"Don't do anything yet," he suggested. "His company is growing. Hit him where it hurts."

Linda decided to take Derek's advice. She'd wait until his business expanded. She watched as Daron purchased real estate properties and invested in stocks and bonds; she kept tabs on all the money he made. However, as Linda and her brother-in-law plotted for her husband's downfall, they developed an attraction for one another and soon became lovers.

Linda wasn't just traveling to attend book launches. She was meeting Derek on almost every occasion.

Even down in the Keys.

She reminisced about those steamy moments and how she sometimes hated herself for betraying her husband with his own brother. But when Derek confirmed that Daron was having yet another affair, this time with a young college girl, it was enough for Linda. All she cared about from that point was Daron's money.

After one last kiss on her precious baby's cheek, she stood back and admired her little bundle of joy.

Baby Lauren did indeed have Daron's eyes, but she knew the truth. Fortunately for Linda, amber eyes ran in Daron's family.

Linda dimmed the light, and as she headed towards their bedroom, she snickered.

Hell. Little Lauren isn't even his baby.

The End